AMISH COVER-UP

ETTIE SMITH AMISH MYSTERIES BOOK 13

SAMANTHA PRICE

CHAPTER 1

*I*t was midmorning when Florence arrived at Lousy Levi's cottage on the edge of his apple orchard. As she raised her hand to knock on his front door, a waft of chilly air swept across the porch and made her neck hairs stand on end. It had been warm earlier that morning and the draft had come out of nowhere, bringing with it a sense of uneasiness. Her hand remained aloft as she gave one final look at the trees in the orchard to one side, and then the contented animals grazing in the fields to the other.

Her visits to Lousy Levi were a duty, not a pleasure. Reminding herself that her late husband would appreciate her taking the time to visit his old friend, she knocked on the door before she changed her mind.

Seconds later, the door was flung open and a disheveled looking Levi stood before her, still fastening one side of his suspenders to the top of his baggy black pants. They had surely seen better days, both he and the pants. Florence didn't know where to look as he finished dressing. Her gaze fell to the ground and then back up into the icy blue of his eyes. His gray hair stood out from his head and the longer, darker strands at the bottom had formed into ringlets.

"Good to see you, Florence. You haven't been here for ages."

"I was here a few weeks ago."

"Seems long ago. Anyway, come in. I'll put a pot of hot tea on for us." He stepped aside and put a hand softly on her arm to guide her in, causing him to stoop over awkwardly.

"Are you sure I haven't called at an inconvenient time? I could come back later if you're in the middle of something."

"Nonsense. I look forward to our talks. No one visits me much anymore."

Florence smiled, knowing why people didn't stop by. He was polite to her, but he wasn't that way with most people. His meanness and poor business dealings had earned him the not-so-nice nickname of Lousy Levi.

After she'd followed him into the kitchen, she sat and waited for him to fill the kettle. He fiddled around with it, tipping some out, and then topping it up again. "It's only just boiled, so it won't take but a moment." When he was satisfied it was at the perfect level, he placed it on the stove and then sat across the table from her.

"I'm glad you came today, because there's something important that you need to know."

"What's that?" Florence asked.

"They're going to kill me, Florrie."

"I keep telling you, Levi, I don't like any shortened versions of my name. Not Florrie, not Flo … Wait a minute. What did you say?" She shook her head, sure she hadn't heard right. "Did you just say some people are going to kill you?"

"That's right. I'm telling you, so you'll know that if I die and it looks like an accident, it won't have been."

"Who's going to kill you?"

The kettle whistled. "Just a moment." He made the tea, let it steep, placed a cup of hot tea in front of her, and then sat back down with a fresh cup for himself.

Florence took a sip. "Who's going to kill you?" Maybe an unpaid worker had threatened him, she thought.

"I'll tell you one person who wants me six-foot-under and that's the old goat next door. He's blaming me because he lost his organic accreditation."

"For his apples?" Florence knew the neighboring property also had apple orchards.

"*Jah.*"

"How did that come about?"

"I use spray and fertilizers and for the last two seasons his fruit didn't test as organic and he said it's my fault. I dunno how these things work. Spray might have gone through the air or the fertilizer seeped through to his land. He's blaming me." He stared at Florence. "Anyway, it's not my problem."

"I can understand why he's upset."

"What has he said about me? Has he said anything to you?"

"Nothing. This is the first I've heard of it. I don't even know the man next door." Florence knew the *Englischer* neighbor by sight, but that was only from seeing him on his property when she'd been visiting Levi.

"How do you know he's upset?"

Florence sighed. "You said someone wants to kill you. He's blaming you, you said, so I figured he'd have to be upset."

"*Jah*, true that."

"Is he that troubled about the whole thing that he'd kill you? It sounds extreme."

"There's more. He wants my land, he does. It'd suit him if I was out of the way. When I go to *Gott*, John will sell out to him. He's got no interest in the orchard. He's a disappointment—not much of a son. Took after his *mudder*, he did."

"Weren't you wanting to sell it too, some years back?"

"*Nee*, I never wanted to sell."

"You did. I remember you were thinking of selling to Tony Troyer."

He shook his head. "You got it all wrong, Florrie."

"Florence!" she corrected him.

"We had plans of going into partnership, but that never worked out."

"Oh." Florence sipped on her tea. It was too far back for her to remember the exact details.

"Just remember, if I die and it looks like an accident, it won't be."

"I'll keep that in mind." Florence stared into her tea while thinking about what she needed at the markets. That was her next stop.

"Why shouldn't I use fertilizers and chemicals if I want? They make the apples look better and taste better."

Slowly nodding, Florence said, "I guess they're your apples."

"That's right. They're my apples and I can do what I want."

"You could try being nice to people though, Levi. You do get off on the wrong foot with people."

He opened his pale blue eyes wide and the fine, web-like veins on the tops of his cheeks got redder. "I'll be nice to people when they're nice to me, and not a moment before."

Florence was taken aback and a little amused at the same time. "I'm just saying that if you think someone's trying to kill you, it could be a good time to rethink how you come across to people."

"You're not listening to me. It's all about the money. It's

not about me and what I'm like. Anyway, I think most people do like me."

Florence stared into her tea, wondering what to say. She didn't find any answers in the cup. No one she knew liked him. They merely suffered him out of a sense of duty because he was a member of their Amish community. He not only treated people in the community roughly, he was unfair to the seasonal workers who came to the orchard, most of whom were *Englischers*.

"How about we have some cookies?" he asked.

Florence looked up. "*Jah*, cookies." He had never offered food when she stopped by. This was a first.

"Wait there. I'll just get 'em." He reached into a cupboard and pulled out a package. When he had placed it on the table, he unwrapped it. "I got this thing earlier today. There are cookies in here." He attempted to open the lid of a nice red cookie box.

"Oh, you didn't bake them?"

He threw his head back and laughed. "I don't bake."

"How did you get the them? They don't look like store-bought cookies."

At that moment, he finally got the lid off and offered her one. "It was easier to open this morning."

She peeked inside to see chocolate covered and chocolate chip cookies. "They look delightful."

"And you're trying to say people don't like me. The cookies landed on my doorstep. I must have a secret admirer."

The chocolate covered one she'd just selected slipped from her fingertips and landed back in the box. "You think someone's trying to kill you and yet you don't mind eating mysterious cookies left at your door?"

"You just said no one likes me, but someone does and these cookies prove it."

That didn't answer her question, and she didn't say that exactly, but she had no energy to inquire further. "I don't think you should eat them if you think someone's out to kill you. You don't even know who left them, do you?"

"I daresay I'll find out soon enough, maybe when I go to the meeting on this Sunday. The cookies might have been left by one of you widows." He gave her a wink, which made her cringe.

"I doubt it." She couldn't stop the words that tumbled out of her mouth.

He wasn't offended and held the box out to her once again. "Aren't you going to have a cookie?"

"*Nee*. I'm suddenly not that hungry."

"Suit yourself." He took a cookie and bit into it. "These are delicious as usual." Crumbs tumbled out of his mouth.

Florence turned away to avoid seeing the cookie fragments that had made their way into the tangles of his beard. It was a ghastly sight.

"Are you sure you don't want one?"

"I'm fine. I'm meeting some friends for lunch at the markets." That was a slight exaggeration. Yes, she was having lunch at the markets, and the 'friends' were the regular workers at the café. She never went to Levi's house without having another place to go on to. Otherwise, he'd have her stay longer.

"Have one, go on." He pushed the cookie box toward her yet again.

"*Nee denke*."

"Are you worried it will ruin your appetite for your luncheon?"

"Something like that," Florence said. Now she knew there was no truth to his worries about someone trying to kill him, otherwise, he wouldn't be eating the cookies. They did look good, and she was hungry. Just when she was weakening, he put the lid back on, stood, and put them back in his cupboard.

Now Florence was even hungrier. That toasted cheese sandwich and caramel latte would taste extra good when she finally reached the café. She'd done her duty by visiting Lousy Levi. Her late husband would have appreciated it.

"*Denke* for entertaining me today, Levi. I'll leave you to your work and *denke* for the tea."

"Are you going so soon?"

"*Jah*, I've got that lunch appointment, remember?"

"I know. Don't leave it so long to visit me again."

"That's if you're still here." Florence laughed.

"That's right. If I'm still here. If I'm not, you know what to do. You'll tell the cops it wasn't an accident, won't you? I don't want whoever killed me to get away with it. It'll either be the goat next door, the nurse who has been looking after my bad leg, my good-for-nothing son trying to get his hands on the orchard, or Tony Troyer. Mark my words, it'll be one of those four. They all want me dead."

"I doubt they do. Anyway, let's not talk about things like that. I'd rather leave on a happy note."

Levi chuckled, and together they walked out to Florence's buggy. "It's a quiet time of year for me, Florence, so stop by anytime."

"I'll do that. Goodbye, Levi." She climbed into her buggy and took hold of the reins. Just as she was about to click the horse onward, Levi coughed hard and then clutched at his throat. Swinging around, she asked, "Are you okay, Levi?"

He nodded and said with a gravelly voice, "Just something caught in my throat." He cleared his throat again and then gagged.

She waited for a moment. "Better?"

"You go on, I'm fine. I'll just get a glass of water."

She clicked the horse onward and just as she was halfway

down his driveway, she stopped the buggy and looked back. She had to make sure he was okay, so she turned the buggy around.

Florence got out of the buggy and stood at the back door, which was the door closest to the kitchen. "Levi!" Strangely, there was no answer. Thinking he could be in the living room, she opened the door and walked into the house. "Levi?" She jumped with fright. He was lying face down in the hallway. Screaming, she ran to him and turned him over. Tapping him on the face, she called out his name. He was alive, but not responding.

He groaned. His mouth opened and she was certain he was trying to speak. Then his eyes rolled back in his head and his body went limp. Florence jumped up and ran to the phone in his outside office area. Her hands shook, but she managed to steady them enough to dial 911. After she told the operator what had happened, she gave him the address and ended the call despite the operator still talking. She had to get back to Levi.

Staring at his lifeless body, all she felt was helplessness and despair. He was gone and there was no way to bring him back. Why hadn't she listened to him more? Perhaps she could've found the time to visit more often, especially since he had no one else.

Wiping away a tear as she leaned over his body, she wondered who would miss him. His wife had died many years ago and they'd only had the one son, and he was estranged and living outside of the community.

Oh, Levi, I've been a bad friend. I should've visited you more often, cooked you the occasional meal, and been more of a friend.

She leaned over and put her head against his chest, hoping to hear any sign of life. There was nothing. She placed two fingers to his neck to feel for a pulse, but there was none.

CHAPTER 2

t was several minutes after Florence had called emergency services before the paramedics arrived. She hurried out the door to lead them to where Levi was, hoping her instincts were wrong and they could revive him.

Two of the paramedics tried to bring him back while a third took her outside and sat her down on a porch chair. She described to him what had happened and Levi's gagging action and the way he'd coughed.

"One minute he was here and the next minute he was gone." It all seemed unbelievable. When she saw a police car heading toward the house, it jogged her memory of him saying he'd be killed. "Someone murdered him." She hurried to the police officers despite the paramedic suggesting she should stay put. "He's been murdered," she blurted out to the policeman who'd just stepped out of the passenger side of the car.

"Did you place the call?" the officer asked.

"Yes."

"We have the deceased's name as Levi Hochstetler."

"Well, he's not dead yet. There's still hope. They're working on him now. That's his name, though."

"And your name?"

"Florence Lapp."

"I'm Officer Burns and this is Officer Skully. What is your relationship to Mr. Hochstetler?"

"A friend. I stop by from time to time to see him. He was fine and then ... he just died. He told me it would happen. He told me if he died it wouldn't be an accident, even if it looked like one. He told me there were people who wanted him dead."

The officers looked at one another. Then one pulled out a notepad and pen. She gave her address, and answered a few other questions that seemed totally irrelevant. "He's been murdered," she told them again.

Officer Burns frowned. "What makes you say that?"

"I was here with him for several minutes this morning and he told me that if he died under suspicious circumstances that meant he was killed. He was most insistent that I tell the police it wasn't an accident."

"But weren't you with him when he died?" The officers exchanged glances again as though she were crazy.

"Not exactly. I was saying goodbye to him and it was as though he was choking, and then as I started down the driveway he said he needed to get a glass of water. Something made me turn around and check on him. I know! It was the cookies! The cookies were poisoned." Florence clutched at her throat. "I very nearly ate one. Please find out if they've been able to revive him."

Skully stayed with her while Officer Burns went into the house. A few minutes later, he came out and when he locked eyes with Florence, he shook his head.

"Could you come down to the station and make a full statement?"

"That would be a good idea."

Officer Skully looked at the buggy. "Is that yours?"

"Yes, it is."

"Do you have anyone you'd like to come to the station with you?"

"A husband, perhaps?" Burns asked.

"My husband is dead." She glanced over her shoulder back to Levi's cottage. "What's going to happen to Levi now?"

"He'll be pronounced dead officially," said Skully.

"You have reason to believe he was killed?" asked Burns once more.

"I do. He told me himself someone was going to kill him for his money."

"Excuse us a minute." The two officers walked a couple of paces away, and then she heard Burns say to Skully, "Call Kelly."

Skully nodded and headed to the police car.

Burns walked back to her. "Why don't you leave your buggy here and we'll have an officer take you to the station?"

"*Nee*, I can drive the buggy there."

"You've had a nasty shock."

"I'm fine. If you don't mind, I'll wait and talk to Detective Kelly myself."

He raised his eyebrows. "You know Detective Kelly?"

"I do."

"We'll still need a statement."

"I understand. I'll wait for him."

While Florence waited, she saw many people coming and going. One man arrived in white coveralls and she hoped he was the medical examiner.

At last, Kelly arrived. Just as he opened his car door, the

two officers, Skully and Burns, had words with him. They were talking about her, she thought, and it was confirmed when Kelly looked over at her. After he finished talking to the officers, he closed his car door and walked over to her. "You're Ettie and Elsa-May's sister, right?"

"Correct."

"I met you before when your house burned down. Your gun was missing and—"

"Yes, that's right. Something like that is hard to forget."

"I can imagine. No need to get your sisters involved in all this."

"The cookies!" Florence said.

Kelly frowned at her. "The what?"

"He died after he ate the cookies." She looked back at the house and started walking to the porch.

"You can't go in there just yet."

Florence stopped still and turned to face Kelly. "They're in the top cupboard in a box. He said someone left them on his doorstep." She clutched at her throat. "I very nearly ate one."

Kelly put both his hands up. "Wait here, please." She sank onto the top step.

When he finally came out, he said, "There'll be an autopsy."

"Isn't there always when someone is murdered?"

He sighed. "Yes. Even when murder is suspected."

"That's what I meant."

"I'll drive you to the station, so we can record your statement."

"I've got my buggy."

He pressed his lips firmly together. "How about I follow you to your house, and then we can go from there? I'll even have someone drive you home again."

She slowly nodded. "I haven't had anything to eat. I was going to have lunch before I did my weekly shopping."

"I'll call ahead and have something ready for you at the station."

"That's very kind of you."

Kelly smirked. "I know."

"A toasted cheese sandwich and a caramel latte?"

"Humph. I think that could be arranged."

"Well, don't follow me too close behind in case I have to stop suddenly."

"I understand. On second thought, I'll have Officer Simons follow you instead and he'll bring you in to the station." Florence stared at him. "That way I can supervise your food delivery."

Her face softened into a smile. "Perfect."

AFTER FLORENCE HAD CALLED the bishop of the Amish community to let him know what had happened, she ate her toasted sandwich and caramel latte in the barren gray interview room. The bread was white and had no flavor. It wasn't nearly as nice as the sourdough bread she was used to from her regular café. She'd have to delay her lunch plans until the next day. The coffee, on the other hand, was passable, but only just. It could've done with more of a caramel flavor.

Detective Kelly walked in. "Nearly finished, I see?"

"Yes, delicious. Thank you."

"Do you have any objection to this interview being recorded?"

"No, none at all."

"Good. I've got a few questions to ask you."

"About who killed Levi?"

"If you don't mind, we'll start with your name. State your full name and address for the record."

She told him what he wanted to know, and that was everything from the time she got to Levi's house until the time she left. "It had to be the cookies." She drained the last mouthful of latte.

"Thank you. We'll have this typed out and you'll need to sign it. That's all we need from you today."

"But you haven't even asked me about Levi's enemies. He's got quite a few."

"If we find he's been murdered, we'll get you back in and ask you more questions. It's only early in the process."

Florence opened her mouth to speak.

"You weren't about to leave town, were you, Mrs. Lapp?"

"No, I wasn't. But don't you want to know while it's still fresh in my mind?"

Kelly sighed. "From the size of the man, it was probably just a heart attack."

"And is that your medical opinion, Detective Kelly? I didn't know you'd been to medical school as well as police school."

"Well, I haven't. That's what the initial findings indicate."

"I think I should tell you about all his enemies."

Detective Kelly glanced at his watch. "How many did you say he had?"

"These are all the people he mentioned to me: the nurse; the man next door who was angry with him; his son who wanted his money; and the man he was going to go into business with, but decided not to. That was many years ago, though, so it probably wasn't him."

"I see. And did Mr. Hochstetler have a lot of money? Was he a man of wealth?"

"Not that I know of, but he had the orchard."

"Ah yes, the apple orchard."

"That's right."

"If we need to know any more about any of those people,

I'm sure you'll be able to tell us all about them. Thank you for coming in, Mrs. Lapp."

"Is that it?"

"Yes, but as I said, we could very well have questions for you later."

By his attitude, Florence knew Kelly didn't think Levi had been murdered and was merely following routine procedure, covering his bases just on the off chance that Levi had been murdered. "I don't think you've been very thorough."

"You've told me everything in minute detail from the time you arrived there today until the time the paramedics arrived, haven't you?"

"Yes, except you don't seem very interested in the people who might have killed him."

"I've got other cases, Mrs. Lapp. If I need to know more, I promise you, you'll be the first person I'll call. For now, it's all under control."

"When will you find out what killed him?"

"Possibly later today. I'll let you know."

"Will you? I don't have a phone anymore. I did have one in the barn, but the phone company kept overcharging me, so I told them I wouldn't pay the outrageous amount they wanted and they disconnected it."

"I'll stop by your house and give you an update. How's that?"

"I'd like an update as soon as you know anything. I was the one who found him lying there. It's been very stressful." Florence wiped a tear from her eye. She normally wasn't one to cry, but it had been an emotional day.

"I know it has. It was unfortunate you were there when he died. I'll have someone drive you home."

"Thank you."

IT WAS a different officer from the one who had followed her buggy to her house and then driven her to the police station. Instead of telling him where she lived, Florence gave the officer Ettie and Elsa-May's address. If anyone knew what to do about the situation she'd found herself in, it would be them.

CHAPTER 3

*E*lsa-May had finally taken her small fluffy dog, Snowy, out for his daily walk. Ettie settled down on the couch with a cup of hot tea. Her favorite time of day was whenever Elsa-May was out of the house. She liked to use the fine bone china teacup that Elsa-May had given her for Christmas. She'd told her oldest sister it was the nicest thing she'd ever seen and she'd meant it. She brought the cup to her lips, holding it with both hands, and hesitated before she took that first sip.

What were those sounds? She listened hard with delight. Silence!

There were no annoying knitting needles clicking together, no slurping of tea, no talking about nothing in particular, and no Snowy pawing on her leg to get up on the couch.

Just as she took a sip of the hot liquid, a loud knock on the door shattered her treasured alone time. The suddenness of the noise had caused Ettie to slop tea down the front of her white apron. She was fuming that Elsa-May had come back too early and startled her like that. Neither of them ever locked the door, so why was her sister knocking at all, let alone so loudly?

Angry words formed in Ettie's head. She was going to let Elsa-May know exactly what she thought of her. Before she had time to get off the couch to confront her, the door opened and someone stuck her head through. It wasn't Elsa-May at all, but it *was* her sister.

"Florence!" Florence was one of Ettie and Elsa-May's sisters. She used to live a distance away but had moved closer so she could live next door to a good friend of hers, Morrie. Ettie suspected that one day they'd marry, but nothing had been mentioned. Was Florence there to tell them a wedding was finally going to take place?

"Ettie, you'll never guess what happened." She rushed toward Ettie and, seeing the cup of tea balanced in her hands, took it from her and placed it on the saucer on the small table beside her.

And just like that, the few precious moments that Ettie only got once a day were ruined and forever lost.

"What is it, Florence?"

"It's Levi. He's dead."

"Lousy Levi?"

"*Jah.* He died today. I was there."

Ettie gasped. "*Nee!*"

"I was. And what's more, he told me if he was to die, that he would've been killed. Someone was out to get him and he knew it. He tried to tell me and I kind of laughed it off and paid him no mind, but it wasn't a joke because where is he now?"

"Dead."

"That's right."

"Who killed him?" Ettie asked.

"He had a list of people who wanted him dead. Well, four of them, so it wasn't a long list."

Ettie rubbed her forehead. "Let's go back to the beginning. You were with him today?"

"*Jah.*"

"Where?"

"At his *haus.* As you know, I visited him every few weeks because I don't think anybody else did. You remember that he was my husband's friend, don't you? Just like he usually did, he made me a cup of tea, and when we sat down and I started drinking the tea, he told me that he thought someone was going to kill him."

Ettie shook her head. "I should've asked this first. How did he die?"

"They don't know for sure, but it had to be poison." Florence told her exactly how things had played out. "I've just come back from the police station. Your nice Detective Kelly made me a sandwich and a cup of coffee and I told him all about it."

"You had to make a statement?"

"*Jah*, and now there's an autopsy and they're testing the cookies too."

"Cookies? What cookies? You never mentioned cookies."

"Didn't I? That's the most important part. He had cookies. He said someone left them on the step outside his front door, and he tried to make me eat one. I wouldn't, and I was shocked that he did since he thought someone was going to kill him."

"He might've been thinking someone was going to shoot him with a gun, or something like that. He might not have thought of poison," Ettie said.

Florence looked around. "Where's Elsa-May?"

"She's out walking Snowy. She should be back soon."

"Your nice detective asked me not to bother you, but you'd find out that Levi died. Everyone will know soon and it would be weird of me not to tell you, wouldn't it?"

"Of course it would. You say they're testing the cookies?"

"They are."

Ettie nibbled on a fingernail. "He was the type of man to have a lot of enemies."

"No one liked him," Florence said.

Ettie slowly nodded. "He was so cranky all the time."

"And he cheated people, but he always had an excuse to justify it to himself."

"So I've heard." Ettie looked longingly at her hot tea, which was growing cold.

"He didn't know how to make friends. I don't know how his wife put up with him for all those years. Or how my husband ever came to be his friend."

When Elsa-May came back from her walk, she was surprised to see Florence. Elsa-May let Snowy go and he ran over to Florence to say hello.

"Hello, Snowy." Florence leaned down and ruffled his furry head.

"Elsa-May, Lousy Levi's dead," Ettie told her.

"He was murdered," Florence added.

Elsa-May's jaw dropped open. Florence filled her in on everything that had happened.

"Did the police say they think it's suspicious?" Elsa-May leaned down and unclipped Snowy's lead, and, satisfied with having received attention from their visitor, the dog went to his bed in the corner of the room.

"They're doing an autopsy," Ettie said, "which is proof that they think there is a possibility it was murder."

"Did John want an autopsy?" Elsa-May sat down in her usual chair.

Florence tipped her head to the side. "John?"

"His son," Ettie said to Florence.

"Oh, right. I'd forgotten that was his name. I haven't talked to him. I called the bishop from the police station. He would be tracking him down. Detective Kelly suspects that Levi had a heart attack because of his size. He said that was the medical examiner's initial findings without doing the full autopsy thing. When I told the detective that Levi said someone was going to kill him, that made him investigate further."

"It's too much of a coincidence that he thought he was going to be killed and then he died on that very day," Ettie said.

"Who would've benefited from his death, Florence?" Elsa-May asked.

"I don't think you're asking the right question," Ettie said to Elsa-May.

"What are your thoughts, Ettie?" Florence asked.

"Levi angered so many people and maybe that's why he was killed, out of hate or out of revenge."

"Good point," Elsa-May said. "As well as finding someone who benefited, we also need to look at who he had wronged."

Florence shook her head. "We could come up with an awfully long list."

"Let's just wait and see what the autopsy turns up, shall we?" Elsa-May asked. "That would be the smart thing to do. No point wasting effort and time."

Florence looked between the two of them. "So does that mean you'll both help me?"

"Help you to do what?" Elsa-May blinked rapidly.

"Find out who killed Levi, of course."

"That's what the police do," Elsa-May said. "Detective Kelly doesn't like it when we interfere."

Florence pouted. "You've done it before."

"But only when we … only when …"

"What Ettie is trying to say is that sometimes Kelly asks for our help. Other times, we just slipped into things by accident."

Florence pressed her back into the chair. "You won't help me?"

"We're not saying that. Why don't we just wait and see what the testing results are?" Elsa-May picked up her knitting from the bag by her feet.

"I suppose that's the most sensible thing to do." Florence nodded.

"Exactly," Elsa-May agreed, popping her knitting glasses onto her nose.

When Florence finally left just before dinnertime, Ettie was bothered by the whole thing. "What do you make of it all?"

Elsa-May continued to click her knitting needles together. "He could have died from natural causes. He was old and he was overweight. The doctor had to give me a stern warning about carrying too much weight, remember?"

"*Jah*, and you have lost a little bit of weight since then."

"A little? I've lost quite a few pounds. Several in fact."

Ettie stared at her, wondering from where those pounds had been shed.

Elsa-May now glared at Ettie over the top of her glasses. "Don't you think so?"

"Undoubtedly," Ettie said, not daring to disagree with her older sister. "I wonder if he died from natural causes or whether somebody did him in."

"As we said before, if he *was* killed there would be a long line of suspects. It might be hard to figure out who did it."

"I know. I remember going back years ago there being complaints that he never paid his workers fairly."

Elsa-May chuckled.

"It's not funny."

"He'd tell them he'd pay a certain amount and he'd never give them that amount."

"I know. He was dreadful like that," Ettie said.

Elsa-May nodded and kept knitting. She was so practiced at it that she never had to look at what she was doing until she got to the end of the row. "The worst thing was that he gave Amish apple growers a bad name."

"Who will take over his orchard?"

"John, I guess. John's his only relative—that I know of, anyway."

A FEW DAYS LATER, Ettie was again settling herself down with a cup of hot tea. She went through the same ritual that she normally did when Snowy and Elsa-May were on their daily walk. She listened carefully to the beautiful sounds of silence and wholeheartedly appreciated hearing nothing at all. Slowly, she brought the cup up to her lips ... and then Florence burst through the door without even knocking.

"There you are, Ettie. You'll never guess what happened."

Ettie managed to get the cup onto the saucer before spilling any of her tea. "What happened?"

"That detective friend of yours came to see me and told me ..." She slumped onto the couch right beside Ettie. "He told me about Levi."

"What did he say?"

"He said Levi died of natural causes. Heart disease, that's what they said. They released his body and he's gone to the funeral home."

"Is John organizing all that?"

"*Nee.* John will be here tomorrow. He's staying at his *vadder's haus* when he gets here. I suppose it's his now. The bishop's organizing the funeral."

Ettie said, "So Lousy Levi wasn't killed at all, like he thought he would be?"

"I still think he was."

Ettie frowned at her sister. "The autopsy would've picked it up if he'd been killed."

Florence pouted. "Is Elsa-May walking Snowy again?"

"*Jah*. I'm surprised you didn't drive your buggy past her."

"She must be walking a different way from the way I came. I'm bothered, Ettie. I'm really bothered."

"About thinking he was killed?"

"*Jah*. What if there was something in those cookies to bring about a heart attack?"

"Is that possible?"

"I'm not sure."

"Did you ask Kelly?"

"*Nee*, he hasn't got the results of the cookies back yet. I was hoping you might talk with him for me."

Ettie couldn't think of anything worse. Kelly hated it when they interfered on one of his cases. "Me?"

Florence nodded.

"I keep away from Detective Kelly as much as possible."

"I thought you two were friends."

"He asks for my help once in a while and that's it. We didn't part on the best of terms last time we saw one another."

"I know he'd take things far more seriously if you were involved. I think that's the only reason he ordered an autopsy."

"Why's that?"

"Because I said I thought he'd been murdered and I repeated what Levi told me right before he died. And because he knows I'm your *schweschder*. That's probably the only reason he believed me. Otherwise, I'm just a silly old lady. To him, I wasn't a silly old fool because I'm your *schweschder*, don't you see that?"

Ettie picked up her teacup, and sighed when she imagined the slightly bored stare Detective Kelly would offer her if she were to talk with him about Lousy Levi's death. He would lower his head with his eyes fastened onto hers, and then his lips would be downturned into a frown, causing deep lines to form between his nose and the corners of his mouth.

Florence took Ettie's tea away from her, set it down, and took hold of her hand. "Will you do it for me, Ettie?"

Ettie covered her eyes with her spare hand. "If you really want me to, I will." What hope did she have, being the youngest child with older siblings to boss her about? Even at their current ages she felt the weight that the youngest child must forever carry. It was all about the pecking order.

"*Denke.* Now I'll make myself a cup of tea since you didn't offer." Florence bounded to her feet and set off toward the kitchen.

"I would've made you one. I didn't have the opportunity because you were telling me something important and holding my hand too tightly."

"There's never an excuse for poor manners, Ettie."

Ettie smiled as she remembered those words of her dear mother's that Florence had just repeated. She could very well have reminded Florence that most people knock and wait to be let in to someone's house before they walk on in with no notice. She gave up, and again picked up her special teacup. The tea wasn't as hot as it would've been if she could have sipped it before she'd been interrupted.

Ettie only hoped she wouldn't have to go alone to see Kelly. If Elsa-May came with her, it wouldn't be so bad.

CHAPTER 4

"*M*rs. Smith and Mrs. Lutz. You don't even have to tell me why you're here. It's regarding your sister and Levi Hochstetler, isn't it?"

"Correct. It is. Our sister is worried about—"

"Come into my office." He spun on his heel and took large strides down the corridor away from the front area of the police station. Ettie and Elsa-May had to hurry to stay close behind. He pushed his door open. "Take a seat."

When everyone was seated and she had caught her breath, Ettie began, "We're dreadfully sorry to bother you and we didn't want to, but Florence is very concerned."

Elsa-May took over, saying, "She's convinced that the cookies in Levi's house were poisoned."

"I can't help that. Just because she's convinced of something doesn't make it so. There was nothing poisonous in the cookies, just the normal cookie ingredients." He lifted a file on his desk. "We just got the report back." He dropped the file and it landed on the desk with a thud. He then tapped his finger up and down on it as he spoke in staccato form as though he were hammering something. "No poison in the cookies."

Ettie licked her lips. If he'd told Florence that as soon as he'd found out, that might have saved her and Elsa-May a trip to see him. "The other thing we were thinking was that there might not have been poison as such, but could there have been something in those cookies that might have brought on a heart attack if the person had heart problems already?"

Elsa-May added, "If the killer had known that he had heart problems."

"I understand what you're saying, but there was absolutely nothing in the cookies. Is that why you're here? Do you want me to have the cookies retested? At the expense of who? Will you pay for it? I appreciate you ladies always helping me in the past when I've asked, but I can't bend the rules. Trust me, there was no poison in the cookies."

"We wouldn't want you to test them again," Ettie said.

Ettie and Elsa-May looked at one another and Ettie wondered what to say next. Without a murder weapon and with the coroner not finding anything suspicious, there was nothing to go on. Kelly always told them he needed evidence and facts, not assumptions or hunches. The word of a dead man who was liked by no one was not evidence.

"It was just a thought. No need to test them again if there was nothing in them the first time, I suppose," Elsa-May said.

"Is there anything else I can help you ladies with?"

Ettie had to do her best to put Florence's mind at rest, and that was to try to uncover anything that might be hidden. "Florence is convinced he was killed. She wasn't with him at the very time he died—well, she was at the end, but not in the moments before. He left her and he went into the house while she started down the driveway, and then she came back."

"What Ettie is trying to say is, what if someone killed him in the house before she got back there? Isn't that right, Ettie?"

"Yes."

"How would someone go about doing that? By giving him a fright?" Kelly asked. "Jumping out and saying, 'Boo'? There was no gunshot wound, no entry point of a weapon. Nothing at all."

Ettie could see it was no use. His mind was made up that there were no suspicious circumstances and that Levi had died of a heart attack, and maybe he was right. Maybe it was Lousy Levi's paranoia that had allowed him to convince Florence that he was killed.

"We'll let our sister know that you've done everything you can to look into his death."

"Good."

"Thank you for your time." Ettie pushed herself to her feet. When Elsa-May started talking, Ettie sat back down.

"The thing is, Detective, he predicted his own death and told Florence he knew that someone was trying to kill him. It sounded like he'd been threatened or he knew someone was out to kill him and he even said it would look like an accident."

"It didn't *look* like an accident at all. There was nothing suspicious and no signs of an accident. The evidence technicians have been through the house collecting evidence and have come up with nothing. Because your sister was so worked up and because of the things she said, an autopsy was done." He shook his head. "That was a monumental waste of time and expense. The cookies were sent off for testing and they were just cookies. Do I need to say again that there was nothing in those cookies?"

"No, we got that," Ettie said.

He rose to his feet. "I suggest that you ladies go back home and put all your concentration into your knitting."

Ettie and Elsa-May stood up and made their way out of the police station.

"What do you think about that?" Elsa-May asked her sister.

Elsa-May held onto the rail of the steps outside the station. "Nothing's changed. He'll never change."

Ettie walked behind her, figuring if she fell, she'd fall on Elsa-May and have a soft landing. "He didn't have to be so rude."

"He's been like that lately. I knew this would be a waste of time." Elsa-May reached the pavement and turned to face Ettie, who'd just stepped down in front of her.

"Not if it puts Florence's mind at rest."

CHAPTER 5

They headed to the pay phone to call for a taxi.

"The only thing we can do is tell Florence what we found out."

"And that's nothing."

"It'll make her feel better."

Elsa-May shook her head. "She was convinced."

The ladies reached the pay phone and stood in front of it as they continued their conversation.

"He was old and he was fat. A good recipe for a heart attack."

"But the two of those don't go together in every case. Many fat people have no health problems whatsoever."

"We've got nothing to go on. If you think someone killed him, how did they do it?"

"Let's, just for the purposes of the argument, say that Levi was killed. That would mean that either the medical examiner made a mistake or the person testing the cookies made a mistake. Mistakes do happen."

"But only in a small percentage of cases, I'm sure."

"Let's ask Florence a few more questions, shall we?" Elsa-

May looked over Ettie's shoulder, stepped closer to the road, and hailed a passing taxi. "This is nice. It saved us a phone call."

THEY KNOCKED on Florence's front door and she opened it.

Her face lit up when she saw them. "Come in."

"We haven't found anything out," Elsa-May said.

Her face fell. "Oh. That's disappointing. I thought that's why you were here."

Elsa-May looked around. "Where shall we sit?"

"Come through to the living room."

Once they were seated, Florence asked, "What happens now?"

"We visited Detective Kelly and he was no use, no use at all. He just kept saying it was a heart attack. 'No poison in the cookies,' he said."

"And maybe it was." Elsa-May placed her hands in her lap.

"You should've heard Levi, though. He kept on, and on, and on about it. He kept saying, 'If I die and it looks like an accident, it's not an accident. I'm trusting you to tell the cops.' And you know he didn't have many friends. I was about his only friend. If I don't do this last thing for him, who will?"

"And he had a lot of enemies," Ettie said.

Florence nodded. "And it was one of them, most probably, who finally killed him."

"When you went back into the house the second time, did you see anything suspicious? Did it look like someone had just been there and left?" Elsa-May asked.

"I didn't even think of that. I was just thinking of Levi and trying to bring him around. It was very frightening. Then he died right there. I was only with him for a few seconds, then he died, and then I ran to call 911 hoping they might be able to revive him."

"Do you have a pen and paper?" asked Ettie

"I do somewhere." Florence got up and opened a bureau drawer and handed her a pen and paper. "What's it for?"

"Sit down," she said to Florence who was standing over her. Once Florence sat down again, Ettie said, "I'm making a list of all the names he mentioned that day, his last day."

"Very well. To start with, there was the man next door. He was very angry with him because—"

"At this stage, don't tell us why they were angry with him. Just tell us all the names he mentioned." Elsa-May spoke in her usual abrupt oldest-sister tone.

Florence didn't seem to notice, or if she did, didn't take offense. "Very well then. There was the man next door, there was his son John, and the nurse that he seemed to be upset with, and the man he was thinking of going into business with years ago; I forget his name now. It's on the tip of my tongue."

"Don't worry. We can find that out," Elsa-May said.

Ettie looked down the list. "The man next door, the nurse, his son, the man he was in business with years ago."

"Is that all?"

"They are the only people he mentioned. He was only *thinking* of going into business with that man. It never actually happened."

"You said that already." Elsa-May turned and said to Ettie, "This all could be a big waste of time."

Ettie pressed her lips firmly together. "You don't have to be involved. You can go back to your knitting like Kelly suggested. It's not as though we've got anything else to do with our time these days."

Elsa-May sighed. "I just hope this is not all for nothing."

"I know how you feel, Elsa-May, and I wouldn't be bothering the both of you with it, but Levi was so insistent with me. He begged me for my help if something happened to him. And now that something has, I owe it to him to look into it. And you're right, it might come to nothing, but on the other hand ..."

"Okay, okay. Let's do this." Elsa-May looked over Ettie's shoulder at her list.

"Let's start with the man next door, shall we?" Ettie suggested.

"The man next door was upset with Levi because he lost his organic farming accreditation because Levi used so much fertilizer and sprays, and of course those things weren't compatible with what the next-door neighbor was trying to do."

"I can see how that would be a problem," Ettie said. "That would've crushed his business."

"He would've lost his customers, I suppose. Did Levi feel bad about that?" Elsa-May asked Florence.

Florence's eyes grew wide. "Not in the least."

Ettie chuckled. "No wonder they didn't get along."

"Then there's his son, John, and he said John will get it all when he goes."

"And I'm guessing he didn't get along with his son in the past few years?" Ettie asked.

"John left the community, as you know. Levi wasn't very welcoming anytime John tried to visit."

"That doesn't mean John killed him," Elsa-May said.

Ettie ignored Elsa-May's comment. "And the next on the list is the nurse. What do we know about her?"

"I don't know very much about her. I know that Levi had just recovered from a bad leg and the nurse had come to his home a few times. I think it was a severe case of gout. I have no idea why Levi was upset with her, but he was."

"And then there's the man he was going to go into partnership with, but didn't. What do you know about that, Florence?"

"Not a lot. I do remember his name now; it was Troyer. *Jah*, Tony Troyer. I think they had a deal worked out, but from what Levi said, the man couldn't raise the money to buy the share they'd agreed on. From memory, Levi was going to retain a larger percentage."

"That sounds about right. Lousy Levi wouldn't have gone fifty-fifty with anyone." Ettie chuckled.

"Shall we start asking Troyer questions?" Elsa-May asked Ettie.

"I think so. *Nee*, come to think of it, we'll ask the closest people geographically and work our way out. Like starting in the center of a wheel and working our way out to the rim."

"Very good," Elsa-May said.

"*Denke* to the both of you for helping me," Florence said. "I thought that detective friend of yours was going to be good, but then he turned on me."

"He can be quite abrupt and almost rude sometimes," Ettie said. "We very often don't know what mood we'll find him in. I suppose that might be due to the stresses of the job. He works such long hours."

"Tomorrow, we'll visit the neighbor and see what we can find out. Oh, Florence, where's John?"

"He's on his way back here in time for the funeral."

"Who's making all the arrangements then, if not his son?" Elsa-May asked.

"The bishop has looked after it since Levi has no relatives here in the community."

Ettie nodded. "I forgot to tell you that, Elsa-May."

"Both of you can talk to the neighbor. There's no reason for me to be involved. Snowy and I will stay here," Elsa-May said.

Ettie didn't mind who went with her as long as she didn't

have to go on her own. "Will you collect me tomorrow, Florence?"

"Okay, and then we'll see the neighbor together."

"Does he have a name?" Elsa-May asked.

"Of course he does," Florence said with a giggle. "Hmm, I heard it once. His first name starts with 'E.' Errol or Eric, I think. I'll know him when I see him."

∽

NORMALLY, Ettie thought over breakfast, she wouldn't have minded helping Florence, but that meant she'd miss out on the quiet time of day she'd grown used to.

"When are you taking Snowy for a walk?" Ettie had hoped she might have a slice of time to herself that morning, before Florence arrived, but it hadn't happened.

"I'll take him soon. Why?" Elsa-May asked.

"Wouldn't you prefer to go when I come home?"

Elsa-May screwed up her nose. "I might as well go when you're out with Florence."

"Wouldn't it be better to go when I get back?"

"Do you want me to wait until then, Ettie?"

Ettie smiled, pleased that it was that easy. "*Jah*, I would like that. *Denke*."

"*Nee*! I'm not going to wait, because it makes absolutely no sense."

Just then, Ettie heard a buggy.

"Here she is now. Are you ready?"

"*Jah*." As Ettie headed to Florence's buggy, she put out of her mind that her favorite time of day had gone and she'd have to wait another day for a chance to be alone. Ettie climbed into the buggy and asked, "Do we know when the funeral is yet?"

"Not yet. I haven't heard. We could go to Levi's house and see if John's there yet."

"Is that before or after we talk to the neighbor?" Ettie asked.

"We might find out what we can from the neighbor before we attempt to talk with John. I'm sure he'll stay at his father's house."

"Good idea."

Ettie settled back in the buggy. It was nice going in a buggy for a change. Because she and her sister lived in a small house with very little land, they didn't have a buggy. People in the community collected them for meetings, and when they were running their own personal errands, they traveled by taxi. As Florence hummed a hymn, Ettie closed her eyes and enjoyed the rumbling sounds of the buggy wheels and the rhythmic clip-clopping of the horse's hooves while a gentle breeze tickled her face.

"Ettie, Ettie."

Ettie felt someone poking her in the shoulder. She'd fallen asleep. She straightened up and looked around. They were near Levi's orchard. "Oh, I don't know what's wrong with me. I had enough sleep last night."

Florence chortled. "Never mind. We're here now."

Ettie looked around again as she woke more fully. "Do you have a plan? What are you going to say?"

"I haven't thought about it yet."

"Quick, think about it now before we go in. We can't ask him if he gave Levi a batch of poisoned cookies, or if he killed him, so what are we going to say?"

"I'll think of something."

Both ladies stepped down from the buggy, and then Florence strode toward the neighbor's house with such a sense of purpose that Ettie guessed her sister had already figured out something to say.

Ettie hurried to catch up. "Have you remembered his name at least?"

"His first name is Eric."

When they got closer to the house, they saw a man to one side painting a section of the porch. He looked up at them and carried the paintbrush as he walked toward them. "Hello."

"Hello. Are you the owner here?"

"I am. Who's asking?"

"I'm Florence Lapp and this is my sister, Ettie Smith."

He looked from Florence to Ettie and then back to Florence. "Is this about Levi?"

"It is. I wonder if we might take a moment of your time."

"I'm listening." He looked down and held the paintbrush out. "I'll just put this aside for now." He went around the side of the house and came back a few moments later, dusting off his hands on the sides of his pants.

Florence continued as though there'd been no interruption. "I was with him when he died the other day. He mentioned you wanted to buy the orchard from him."

His face lit up. "Is his son going to sell it to me?"

"You'll have to ask him that. I think he's arriving here soon. He's coming for the funeral, of course."

"Well, I've got a complaint about Levi. He took money off me and I need it back. I've been watching and waiting, hoping his son will get here soon, so I can see what he'll do about it."

The news didn't surprise Ettie and she wondered if that was going to be a familiar theme as people gathered, asking to get paid back for Levi's questionable actions. She wouldn't want to be in John's shoes.

At that moment, a red sports car squealed up the driveway of Levi's property next door.

"Could that be John now?" Ettie asked Florence, as the three of them stared at the red car.

When a middle-aged man with a mop of dark hair got out of the car, Florence knew it was John. He was much older than when she'd last seen him. "That's him." A woman got out of the passenger-side door and together they walked up to the front door of the house. "That'll be John's wife, Connie," Florence added. "I'm pretty sure that's her name."

"We should talk to them." Ettie wanted to get away from Eric and find out if John knew about the money Eric had just accused Lousy Levi of taking.

"You better tell them I'll be over to see them before too long as well. I need to get what's owed me."

They said goodbye to Eric and headed over to Levi's house.

Ettie whispered, "We still didn't get his full name, but he got ours."

"Come to think of it, you're right."

CHAPTER 6

*T*he door of Levi's house closed when Ettie and Florence approached.

"Hello," Florence called out when she saw movement through one of the windows.

"Here are the vultures now. It didn't take them long," a woman's voice said from within the house.

They heard a man's voice reply, "Be quiet!" The door opened and John stood there smiling at them. "Mrs. Lapp, and is it … Mrs. Smith?"

"That's right," Florence said.

"Hello, John," Ettie said, "It's been a long time."

"How are you feeling? This must've come as quite a shock for you."

John patted his chest. "It came right out of the blue. I just talked to him a couple of weeks ago." A woman appeared at his shoulder. "Mrs. Lapp and Mrs. Smith, this is my wife, Connie."

They smiled and nodded at Connie.

"It's Florence and Ettie," Ettie said. "I think we can dispense with the formalities now that you're all grown up."

John chuckled. "Ettie and Florence it is. Would you like to come in?"

"No, we won't bother you," Florence said.

He fixed his gaze onto Florence. "They told me you were there when my father died?"

"I was. It happened quite suddenly—out of the blue, like you said."

"If you don't mind me asking, what were his last words?"

"His last words, or his last conversation?"

Ettie stepped forward. "He was disturbed and spoke about some enemies he had."

Florence whipped her head around and stared at Ettie. "Ettie!"

Ettie knew Florence was disappointed, but where would they get if they sugar-coated everything? Besides, the father and son weren't close.

He gave a small laugh. "It's okay. My father always had enemies. He didn't have many friends. I think you were his only friend anymore, Florence."

Florence exhaled deeply. "I kept telling him he needed to be more friendly with people, but he also had a problem with listening."

"I want to thank you for keeping him company the way that you did."

"I didn't do much. I only visited him every now and again. I should tell you that the man next door seems particularly unhappy. He's talking about a debt he needs to settle with you or something. No doubt he'll stop by to see you soon."

John rolled his eyes. "I was expecting this kind of thing. The bishop told me of two people already who've got their hands out."

"Did your father have a lot of money?" Ettie asked.

Florence was visibly shocked. "Ettie, you don't ask things like that!"

"I was hoping he had a lot if John has to pay people back, that's all."

John chuckled. "It's okay. I'm not offended or anything. I don't know the specifics of my father's finances. I'm just hoping I don't have too many problems with the folks around here."

Connie took a step forward. "If you'll excuse us, we've had a very long drive and we'd like to rest."

Florence stepped back. "Oh, I'm sorry. Well, we might talk to you at the funeral then, John."

"Yes, we'll talk then. I'll walk you to your buggy." When they were nearly at the buggy, he said, "I'm sorry for what my wife said about vultures. I know you heard her. She's got it in her mind that my father was worth a lot of money. I suppose I'll get quite a bit for the orchard, that is, if he left it to me. I still don't know what's in his will."

"He had no one else to leave it to, so he would have left the orchard to you," Florence assured him.

"Maybe, or he could have left it to a charity, or someone in the community. I'm not assuming anything."

When they got to the buggy, Florence stopped still. "I wasn't going to say this because I didn't want to upset you, but your father was convinced that someone was trying to kill him. He specifically said that if he died and it seemed like an accident, it wouldn't have been and he would've been killed."

"That's an odd thing for him to say. Anyway, it wasn't an accident. They told me it was a heart attack."

"I know, but it seemed odd that the very day he was telling me all this he died—on that same day. Just moments later, really."

John rubbed his chin.

"He'd never mentioned anything like that before?" Ettie

asked. "That someone might be angry enough with him to kill him?"

John drew his dark eyebrows together and looked up at the sky for a moment. "No, never."

"I wonder if someone had threatened him," Ettie said.

Florence shrugged her shoulders. "I don't know. He didn't say anything like that to me."

"When was the last time you talked to him, John?" Ettie asked.

"Only a couple of weeks ago. He was complaining about the nurse taking his money and he wanted me to put in a formal complaint." John laughed and shook his head. "The old man never had much money in the house. It would've been what he'd saved in his cookie jar and that wouldn't have been much."

"Did you complain?" Florence asked.

"No. I said I'd file a complaint, but I didn't. He had no proof and I didn't want to risk the woman losing her job over a misunderstanding. He could've put his money somewhere and forgotten where he put it."

"That's understandable," Florence said.

John rubbed his chin. "Because he was so upset, I eventually got my friend in the police department to see if she had a record. I didn't think she'd have the job of going into people's homes if she'd had one. Turns out, she had no record of a criminal history, but somehow my friend managed to find out she'd had a charge against her some time ago and it had been dropped."

"What charge?" Florence asked.

"Something to do with negligence, I think he said. Because it had been dropped, he couldn't tell me too much about it."

"Did that make you worried about your father?" Florence asked.

"No. What he had wasn't life threatening and he wasn't incapacitated."

"And why did he have a nurse come to the house?" Ettie asked.

"He had a bad leg. Bad circulation due to him being a diabetic."

"I didn't know that diabetes caused bad circulation," Florence said.

"You'd be surprised about all the side effects. I think it was a mixture of that and gout. He was a big drinker."

"I wasn't aware of that," Florence said. "He was never intoxicated when I was visiting."

"I don't know. He might have reformed, then. He drank a lot on my last visit a couple of years back."

"And your father never found out that the nurse had been charged for something in the past?"

"No. He would've made a big deal out of it. I wasn't going to bring the police into it over a handful of change."

"How much was missing?" Ettie asked.

"He didn't say." John glanced back at the house and Ettie could see he was growing impatient and had to get back to his wife.

"We won't hold you up, John."

He smiled at them. "It was nice to see both of you again."

CHAPTER 7

"*A*nother funeral, Elsa-May," Ettie said as she sat down at the breakfast table with her sister on the day of Levi's funeral.

"Are you still convinced he was killed?"

"I never was convinced. It was Florence that was sure he was killed because of what he told her."

"I wonder if anyone would miss us if we didn't go to the funeral," Elsa-May said with a wicked gleam in her eyes.

Ettie gasped. "Don't you want to go?"

"Not especially."

"I think they would miss us, especially Florence. We need to be there to support her. And Jeremiah and Ava would miss us because they're collecting us and taking us there."

"I know." Elsa-May hunched her shoulders, picked up a piece of toast, and munched on it.

"If you don't feel like going, stay here. I'll go instead for the both of us."

"I suppose I should go. It's just a little bit depressing now that I've gotten to my age. At every funeral I go to, I wonder if mine will be next."

"One time you'll be right."

"*Denke.*"

Ettie looked across at her sister to see her glum face. "What does it matter? We've lived a long time and everyone's got to go sometime. It'll just be like moving to another *haus.* A bigger and better one. He says He has created mansions for us. It's got to be bigger than this small place." Ettie chuckled.

"That will be something to look forward to. Although, I like this little *haus.* And what will become of Snowy? He's only a young dog, so I'll probably go before he does."

"Don't worry about Snowy. He's the last of your problems."

"Okay, let's just think about this for a moment. If I die tomorrow, what would you do with Snowy?"

"He can go back to the dog shelter he came from."

"Ettie!" Elsa-May gasped. "You wouldn't do that, would you?"

Ettie chuckled. "Of course not. I'm only teasing you. I'll look after him and he'll become my dog. He's always liked me better anyway."

Elsa-May's brow furrowed. "What makes you say that?"

"Do you remember why we put his dog bed in the corner over there?"

"Because he likes to keep warm by the fire."

"*Nee.* He likes it there because he's closer to me."

"Well, if he likes you better, then perhaps you should take him for a walk every day."

"I was only joking. Of course he likes you better and always has. Anyway, it's good for you to get some exercise."

"It would be just as good for you even though you don't need to lose any weight. I don't know how you've always managed to stay so stick-thin."

"I don't eat much."

"You eat the same amount as I do."

Ettie knew her sister ate three times the amount she did. A change of subject was needed. "I wonder if Detective Kelly will be at the funeral."

"He won't. Florence said he wiped his hands of the whole thing. He said Levi died of natural causes. He'd be too busy to go to every funeral in town."

"Who do you think will be there?"

"Not many people, that's for sure and for certain. It'll just be the bare minimum of the community members who go to all the funerals. There won't be a big turnout."

Ettie drained the last of her tea. "I think you might be right."

"You will look after Snowy after I'm gone, won't you?"

"You know that I will."

"It seems to me that you think I'll die first?" Elsa-May asked.

"It only makes sense that you would. You're the oldest. Now hurry along. Jeremiah and Ava will be here soon. You know how Jeremiah doesn't like to be kept waiting."

"I'm always ready on time."

Ettie made a start of clearing the breakfast dishes off the table. "Don't let today be any different. Look! I'm dressed and ready to go and you're still in your dressing gown." Ettie tilted her head to one side. "Are you okay?"

"I'm fine. It won't take me long to get dressed, just two minutes." Elsa-May stood and walked out of the room.

"Hmmm, we'll see."

Jeremiah said he would come to collect them at ten minutes to ten. Right at that time, Ettie looked out the window and saw Jeremiah and Ava's buggy heading toward the house.

"They're here, Elsa-May." Ettie heard loud coughing coming from her sister's bedroom. "Are you okay?"

"I think I'm getting a cold. I should stay home."

49

Ettie peeped into Elsa-May's bedroom to see her still in her dressing gown. *"Jah,* you should if you're not feeling well."

"I'll stay; you go on ahead."

"You made no effort to get ready."

Elsa-May looked up at her. "That's because I'm not feeling well."

"Do you want me to stay here and look after you?"

"Nee, you go and tell me about it when you get back."

"Are you sure?"

Elsa-May nodded and then wiped her nose with her handkerchief. *"Jah.* You go."

"Do you want me to bring anything back for you?"

Elsa-May shook her head. "I'll stay here and have a rest."

"Okay."

"You better go now because Jeremiah is waiting. Bye. Have a nice time."

"I'll try."

Ettie pulled on her black over-bonnet over her white prayer *kapp.* Then she pulled on her black cape. "Have a nice time?" she muttered, thinking about her sister's words. You couldn't exactly have a nice time at a funeral. After she had closed the door behind her, Ettie made her way out to the waiting buggy.

"Isn't Elsa-May coming?" Ava asked.

"She wasn't feeling too well. She's had a cold and she's getting a bad cough."

"That's not good," Jeremiah said.

"Should I stay with her?" Ava asked.

"She said she was fine and just needed a little rest. And you don't want to catch a cold, do you?" Ettie asked.

"Nee, I don't."

"She'll be fine. She's just had breakfast and we'll be back in a few hours."

Jeremiah turned his horse around and headed back down to the main road. Ettie had a lot to tell Ava, but not while Jeremiah was around. If they discussed what Florence thought to be true, Jeremiah would think they were gossiping. She'd wait until Jeremiah was out of earshot.

CHAPTER 8

"hat do you make of it all, Ettie?" Ava asked after Ettie filled her in on the mysterious events surrounding Levi's death.

"So far, I see no reason to believe that he was murdered. It seems that it's just a coincidence that he was talking to her like that on the very day that he died. And you know that I don't believe in coincidences, so the whole thing unsettles me."

"I think that deep down you agree with Florence."

"Maybe I do."

They walked over to the bishop's house where everyone had gathered, and Florence came out to greet them. They were just about to walk inside when they saw John's red car stop close to the bishop's house.

"I'm going over to speak to him," Florence said as she started walking.

"I'll come with you."

"Not me. I'll go inside and say hello to some people." Ava headed to the house while Florence and Ettie walked over to John, who'd come alone.

"Hello." He nodded to both women. "Things have taken a sour turn and my poor wife is too upset to come out today."

"What's happened?" Florence asked.

"The man next door, Eric Johnston, just dropped a bombshell on us. He told us that he gave my father eighty thousand dollars in cash as a deposit on the land back when he wanted to buy it. He still wants the sale to go through, minus the eighty thousand dollars, of course."

"That's a lot of money."

"He gave Levi cash, you said?" Ettie asked.

"My father didn't trust banks unless he had to."

"Do you believe the man?" Florence asked.

"I don't know. Maybe Levi has got the money hidden around the house somewhere."

"He didn't mention to me that he was thinking of selling," Florence said.

"He told me he was considering it. It was when Eric lost his accreditation. My father told me he came to the house yelling at him. Dad said if he was that upset about it, he could buy him out. Then they struck a deal, which my father probably went back on when he had time to think it through. You see, Dad could've given the money back to Eric for all we know, and now I have no proof. If Dad had returned the money, he wouldn't have given two thoughts about the receipt."

"Does the man next door have proof that he gave your father a deposit?"

John slowly nodded. "Yes. He said he has a receipt signed by both of them. He showed me a copy and left it with me. I'm not sure if it's genuine or not."

"Oh dear," Florence said.

"You got that right. It looks like my father's signature, but he signed it slightly different every time he wrote it. Anyway, I'm putting that out of my mind. Today, I'm saying the final goodbye to my father. I'll handle everything I need to, but later."

The three of them made their way into the house. It was an open casket viewing and when everybody had paid their respects, the coffin was covered over and then it was carried out by six men to the specially made funeral buggy.

Once the funeral buggy was ready to proceed to the graveyard, everyone followed behind it in their buggies, creating one long funeral procession. Although, there weren't as many buggies as usual following along at this funeral. Levi was to be buried in the Amish and Mennonite cemetery, as was the custom for the people in their community.

As Ettie stood at the freshly dug grave with the handful of people who were gathered, she suddenly remembered the nurse. Levi had been upset because the nurse had taken his money. What if it wasn't just the money from the cookie jar —what if Levi had been talking about the eighty thousand dollars?

When the bishop started talking, Ettie made a mental note to raise that with Florence and John later, after the funeral.

The bishop gave a small talk about life and death, and how death was not to be feared, as it was part of the cycle of life. Ettie was again reminded that this earth was not her true home.

When the people dispersed to go their separate ways, Ettie grabbed onto Florence's arm and, making sure no one could hear what was said, suggested that they should look closer at the nurse.

"You think the nurse stole that large amount of money?"

"He had money missing, and he said that the nurse had taken his money. He was so upset about it that he called John even when they weren't getting along."

Florence nodded. "It was odd he didn't call the police when he had that much money missing."

"We're talking about Levi, remember? He might have had some reason why he didn't want to call the police."

Florence rubbed her neck while looking at the ground. "What about the possibility that the man next-door might have made it all up? He might have lied about the money he gave Levi to make up for losing his accreditation. It could've been his way of being compensated—making Levi pay in the end."

"And he went so far as to make a full receipt and forge Levi's signature?"

"Things like that have been done before."

"Why don't we visit him tomorrow?" Ettie asked.

"Okay. What will we say?"

"We'll ask him some more questions."

"What about the nurse?" Florence asked.

"*Jah*, it seems odd that she was charged once. I wonder if she'd been charged for stealing. How could we find that out?"

"Your detective friend could find out," Florence suggested.

Ettie shook her head. "He's not my friend and unless it was his idea, he wouldn't look anything up. Besides, he wouldn't be able to tell us anything so confidential."

"John's policeman friend told him."

"*Jah*, but he shouldn't have and Kelly plays by the rules."

"That's a pity."

Ettie glanced over and saw Jeremiah waiting by his buggy with Ava. "I'll have to go. Shall we say ten tomorrow morning?"

"You're not coming to the meal at the bishop's *haus*?"

"Elsa-May has a cold and Jeremiah and Ava are taking me home early. I'm sure she'll be fine, but I don't like her to be alone when she's feeling ill."

"Okay. I'll be at your *haus* at ten in the morning. *Denke* for helping me with all this, Ettie. I wouldn't have given two thoughts to any of it if Levi hadn't been so insistent that he was going to be murdered."

"I understand. I have a feeling there's more to this whole thing now, too."

"*Jah*, eighty thousand feelings."

Ettie nodded. "Exactly. Something's not right."

AFTER AVA and Jeremiah delivered Ettie to her home, she said goodbye to them, pushed open her door, and then saw Elsa-May sitting in her usual chair, knitting. She still hadn't gotten dressed. Her gray hair was caught up in a long braid that hung down one side of her body.

"How are you feeling?"

Elsa-May looked at her, but didn't answer and her mouth was moving strangely from side to side.

"Are you eating candy?"

The knitting dropped into Elsa-May's lap and she covered her mouth with her hand and then swallowed. "I was, until you interrupted me."

"It's not a good idea for you to have candy."

"I only had a couple of pieces."

"Are you feeling better?"

"A little."

"Or did you just want to stay home and have some peace and quiet and eat things you're not supposed to?"

Elsa-May gave a little laugh. "It wasn't like that exactly."

Ettie couldn't blame her. There were days when she felt like doing nothing at all, too. She took off her over-bonnet and cape and then sat down on the couch beside Elsa-May's chair. "It was an eventful funeral."

"What happened?"

"John was there without his wife—"

"Levi's son was at his funeral?" Elsa-May asked sarcastically.

Ettie ignored her and continued, "Lousy Levi's neighbor told John he gave Levi eighty thousand dollars as a down payment on the orchard. It seems Levi was going to sell the orchard to him. And remember how Levi said the nurse stole the money?"

"I remember you mentioning that. But I had no idea that she stole such a large amount."

"We don't know that she did, not for sure. Everyone imagined it was a small amount Levi was complaining about her stealing, such as forty dollars at most, from the cookie jar."

"So, she could've taken a whole lot more."

"Jah."

"Aren't you back early?"

"I came straight from the cemetery. I was worried about you. If I had known you only wanted a parcel of time by yourself I would've stayed away longer."

"Snowy and I were getting a bit lonely by ourselves. We don't mind you coming back early."

Ettie chuckled. "Florence and I are going to visit the neighbor tomorrow. John said the neighbor produced a receipt signed by Levi as proof of the eighty thousand down payment."

"Levi was selling to the neighbor?"

"He said he would, so the neighbor says. Now the money's missing, and I thought that perhaps that's the money Levi was complaining about the nurse taking."

Elsa-May nodded and Ettie gave a shrug.

"Why wouldn't he have put it in the bank? Surely he wouldn't have left that much lying around."

"That's something we'll never know for sure because Levi's no longer around to ask."

Elsa-May put her knitting back in the bag by her feet.

Ettie asked, "Have you gotten over your depression about dying?"

"I wasn't depressed. I was just talking about it. It's called having a conversation. Nothing to make a fuss about."

"It sounded a little more than that."

Elsa-May laughed.

"And have you gotten over that cold that was coming on this morning? Was it just your idea of a way to have some peace and quiet?"

"*Nee*, but I did want to rest. You're right about that and I feel better now *denke*."

"Do you want to come with us tomorrow?"

"I think two people visiting the neighbor will be quite enough. I don't think it's good to have three of us there. Three's a crowd."

Ettie nodded. That meant Elsa-May would have more free time away from her.

"Well, don't you think so, Ettie?"

"*Jah*, you're right."

"I usually am," she said quietly.

"I just realized you're hiding candy from me."

Elsa-May fluttered her lashes. "I'm not hiding anything."

"When did you get those candies?"

"Last time we went to the store."

"We didn't have candy on the list, and I didn't see any amongst our groceries."

"They were there. I didn't manufacture them out of thin air."

"Can I have one?" Ettie asked.

Elsa-May shook her head. "*Nee.* They're bad for you."

"They're just as bad for you. I feel like a piece of candy right now."

"You'll spoil your appetite, Ettie."

Ettie narrowed her eyes. "You told me you wouldn't eat anything you weren't supposed to."

"Now you're suddenly caring about my welfare and what I'm eating?"

"I always watch out for you. That's why I make sure you go for a walk every day." Ettie sighed. "Just let me have one small piece of candy?"

Elsa-May chuckled. "In the cupboard behind the sugar and don't make a glutton of yourself."

Ettie's face lit up, and she pushed herself to her feet and headed to the kitchen. The sugar was kept on the very bottom shelf. She crouched down and when she reached around behind it she stopped. Suddenly visions of someone replacing the candy with a mousetrap jumped into her mind. She pulled the sugar out and when she saw the tin of candy, she giggled to herself about being so suspicious of her dear older sister. Of course Elsa-May wouldn't have put a mousetrap where she told her the candy would be.

As Ettie stood up, the thought occurred to her that maybe Florence had blown this whole thing out of proportion in her mind. Just a simple comment from Lousy Levi about him imagining someone was going to kill him had made everybody look suspicious, when in reality, Lousy Levi might've died of a heart attack.

"Did you find them?" Elsa-May called out from the living room.

"I did. You had them well hidden," Ettie called out to her sister.

"I was only looking after you."

"I'm sure you were."

Ettie popped a pink and white strawberries-and-cream candy into her mouth and savored the burst of flavor.

CHAPTER 9

*E*ric stepped out on the porch of his house as Florence and Ettie approached. When they got within speaking distance, he asked, "Did *he* send you over?"

"John?" Florence asked.

"Yeah." He looked from one lady to the other.

Florence said, "No. Although he told us about Levi agreeing to sell you the orchard at one point."

"He admitted it?"

Florence shook her head. "No, I'm sorry, he didn't. I'm not sure what Levi said to his son. John said you told him that his father might have been thinking about selling the orchard to you, and that you said you gave Levi an amount of money for a deposit."

"That's right."

"Can I see the receipt if you don't mind?" Ettie asked.

"Yes, you can have a look. I made several copies. I gave one to John yesterday morning. Come inside and I'll show you." He walked into the living room, and invited them to sit down while he looked through some paperwork on a shelf.

"How long ago did this take place?" Ettie asked.

"See for yourself." He grabbed one sheet of paper and handed it to Florence. Ettie moved so she could see what was written on it.

"This is dated a couple of months ago," Florence said.

"There's your answer," he said with a flourish of his hands.

Florence asked, "Levi never told you the money had gone missing?"

"That's not my problem. If he lost the money, that's on him—it's his fault, not mine. I handed it over, and I've got the receipt to prove it. If he chooses to lose it, burn it, give it away, it's not my problem. That was part of the land deal."

"Did you ever sign a contract for the purchase of his land?"

"That was coming. I gave the money to him in good faith. Anyway, if the sale's not going ahead, I'm entitled to get my money back. That's how things work. You tell John I want my money."

"What is it that makes you want to buy the orchard so badly?" Ettie asked.

He sat down again. "I figured that was the only way to get my organic accreditation back. That was the only way I could stop the sprays coming onto my land. Levi was never going to make any attempt to prevent my land from becoming contaminated."

Ettie pressed her lips together. "I don't know anything about apple growing, particularly organic apple growing, but wouldn't it have taken you quite a long time to recoup your money? I'm guessing you can't go from using chemicals, and then the next season you're suddenly organic."

"You're correct. It's a process that will take some years, waiting to get the soil free of contaminants. But I'm dedicated to farming; it's my life. I want to leave any land I own better than when I found it. Yes, I need to make money and make a living, but that's not my primary concern. I'll tell you one thing, though: I can't afford to lose that money. Levi's son needs to cough it up and give it back, or sell me the land minus my deposit."

"You mean sell you the land as though he has the deposit?"

"Of course."

"Why didn't you go down the legal route in the first place, and do a proper contract for the sale?"

"Levi wasn't the easiest man to deal with. I thought I'd tease him with a large cash amount. I thought it would be more tempting to see all the cash with his own eyes, knowing he could have more once the deal was done. I know he had the reputation for being mean, but I never thought he'd be dishonest to that extent." He shook his head. "I can't believe the money's gone missing."

"You never got the police involved?"

"No."

"Have you talked to John about this?" Florence asked.

"I just mentioned we had a conversation about it."

Seeing him look slightly annoyed with Florence, Ettie said, "I think what Florence meant to say was, did you get any indication whether John would sell?"

"I asked him if he would and he said he'd get back to me with a decision as soon as all the legal paperwork was done to get the orchard into his name. That shouldn't take long." He scratched his head in an agitated manner. "I'm just one step away from going to the cops about that money, don't worry about that."

"You don't want to do that at this stage," Ettie said.

"I've got eighty thousand reasons to go to the cops. You tell John I'm giving him three days to agree to sell to me or he can give me my money back."

"Or what?" Florence asked.

"I'll go to the cops, and the media. The newspapers and news stations would like to know how the Amish defraud people."

"One person does not represent the Amish people as a whole. This is an isolated case," Ettie said.

"Twist things any way you want, I don't care. I just want my money back."

Ettie pushed herself to her feet. "We'll talk to John and see if we can work something out."

Florence reached out her hand and Ettie pulled her off the couch

"Thank you to both of you for helping to get this thing sorted."

Ettie walked to the door with Florence close behind her. When she reached the door, Ettie turned around. "Did Levi have many visitors, did you notice?"

"There were often people coming and going. There were casual workers in the picking season. Is that what you mean?"

"What about in the last few weeks? We understand he wasn't too well and had a nurse visiting from time to time," Florence said.

He shrugged his shoulders as he pulled open the door for them. "I don't know anything about it."

"Do you know if Levi had any enemies?" Florence asked.

He threw his head back and laughed. "A man like him probably had nothing but enemies. The question should be, did he have any other friends apart from you, Mrs. Lapp."

Ettie slowly nodded, knowing Lousy Levi wasn't a popular man. "Good day," she said. Both ladies walked out the door and after Eric said goodbye, he closed the door loudly.

lorence and Ettie made their way to John's house and knocked on his door. To Ettie's disappointment, Connie opened the door.

"Might we have a word with John?" Florence asked.

Connie looked them up and down. At last, she stepped aside and said, "Come in." She showed them through to the living room and when they had sat down, she called out to John. "He won't be long," she told the ladies.

"Thanks, Connie," Ettie said.

"If you don't mind, I've got things to do at the other end of the house."

"Of course, don't mind us," Florence said.

They only had to wait a few minutes before John walked into the room and looked surprised to see them. "Hello." He sat down on the armchair opposite the couch where they were seated.

"We just visited Eric," Ettie said.

"You did?"

"That's right. He still wants to buy the land—the orchard."

John tugged on his collar and scratched his neck. "The

will's being read tomorrow at the lawyer's office. I can't do anything more until I know whether my father's left me anything. I assumed he would, but with him, it'd be hard to tell. As you undoubtedly know, he was a difficult man to get along with. I'm his only child and when I left the community we didn't speak for years. Then gradually we started talking. In the end, we'd check in with one another by phone every few months."

"Yes, we know," Florence said.

"For all I know, he might have left everything to you, Florence," John said.

Florence laughed. "*Nee.* We weren't that close. I just stopped by every now and again to see if he needed anything."

Ettie said, "One thing we wanted to talk to you about, John, is the missing money. You said your father complained about money missing. Do you think he might've been talking about the eighty thousand dollars?"

John's cheeks turned beet red. "Surely not! Wow. I never even thought about that."

"It might pay to check into that nurse."

"I got my friend to check her background and she had a criminal history."

Ettie said, "You said your policeman friend found she was charged for something and then those charges were dropped."

"That's right. I should go to the police if we could be talking about that amount."

"It might be a good idea," Florence said.

Connie walked into the room. "What business is this of yours?" She glared at Florence and then turned a little and glared at Ettie.

John stared up at his wife from the armchair. "Connie, they're only trying to help."

She now glared at her husband. "Why?"

"You're right," Ettie said. "It's absolutely none of our business." She pushed herself to her feet, and then said to Florence, "Are you ready to go?"

"Yes."

John stood. "I thank the both of you for helping. I'll go to the police station now and give them the name of that nurse and they can look into the whole thing."

"Very well."

The elderly ladies said goodbye to John and Connie and then left the house.

"She was very rude, Ettie," Florence said when they were a distance from the house.

"I know. I don't know why she had to be so hostile."

"She's probably sick of the sight of us."

They got back into Florence's buggy and then Florence took Ettie home.

"Are you coming inside?" Ettie asked Florence.

"I would, but I remembered I put washing on this morning and I need to hang it out to dry."

When Ettie got back inside her house, Elsa-May was waiting for her with news.

"Sit down, Ettie. I have something to tell you."

Ettie sat down on her usual couch. "What is it?"

"While you were out, I had a visitor, Jennifer Byler. She was concerned about me not being at the funeral and thought I was unwell. Which I was, but I'm better now."

"Go on."

"It turns out that Jennifer knows someone who knows Connie, Lousy Levi's daughter-in-law."

Ettie leaned forward. "And?"

"Connie isn't happy with John because he's a gambler, and he's frittered away their life savings." Elsa-May looked pleased with herself.

"Is that all?"

Elsa-May's lower jaw jutted out. "Don't you see, Ettie? What do gamblers need?"

"Money?"

"How much money?"

"A lot?"

"Exactly." Elsa-May raised a finger in the air. "The last time Lousy Levi was talking to John, wouldn't he have mentioned the money that Eric gave him? Wouldn't he have discussed it with him whether to put it in a bank or leave it there in the *haus* somewhere?"

"Ah, I see where you're going with this. You think John stole the money?"

"He could've taken the money thinking he'd put it back before Levi noticed it missing. He might never have intended to actually steal it in that sense. He would've seen it as borrowing the money hoping to win more, but then maybe he gambled it away and had no way of repaying it."

Ettie nodded. "And he'd have been doing this without Lousy Levi knowing."

"Of course. Lousy Levi would've had no idea," Elsa-May said.

Ettie sighed. "And what if John discovered he could never repay it and then he decided to kill two birds with one stone? If he killed his father and made out someone else stole the money, or perhaps made people think it never existed, John could get even more money by selling the orchard."

"Exactly, but the only thing is, John doesn't seem like a killer."

"No one ever does," Ettie said. "Killers can be just like regular people."

"I guess he never got along with his *vadder*, but that doesn't mean he'd kill him."

Ettie shook her head. *"Nee,* it doesn't seem like it would be true."

"Okay. It was just a thought." Elsa-May shrugged her shoulders. "What did you do today?"

"We visited Eric and then John. Eric showed us a copy of the receipt for the eighty thousand dollars and then we went to John's house, and his wife nearly kicked us out."

Elsa-May's eyebrows rose. "She probably knows he killed his father."

Ettie ignored Elsa-May's suggestion. "We did mention the possibility that the nurse might have taken the money. It had never occurred to him."

"If he's guilty, you've just given him someone else to blame." Elsa-May shook her head. "That poor nurse."

Ettie said, "We don't know anything for sure yet. Connie might be the guilty one."

"I know for sure that I'm hungry."

"I'll make you some soup."

"Denke, Ettie. I'm still not feeling the best."

Ettie put a ham bone in a large pot to boil, then spread out vegetables on the table, and sat down to scrape the skins and cut them into small pieces. As she cut the vegetables, she thought about Lousy Levi and the conditions surrounding his death.

Later, when the soup was simmering, she walked down the road to the shanty where the phone was housed and called Morrie to deliver a message to Florence to come to their place for dinner. If the three sisters put their heads together, they might be able to work some things out.

CHAPTER 11

"*J*ohn will know tomorrow whether he's inherited the orchard," Florence said as she sat down at the table in Ettie and Elsa-May's kitchen.

Elsa-May tucked a paper napkin over the top of her dress and straightened it, smoothing it down against her dress. "And by now, Detective Kelly will know about the nurse and he'll be looking into her background."

Ettie added, "He'll also be able to see whether she deposited a large sum of money into her bank account."

"Surely she wouldn't have been stupid enough to put it into her own bank account," Florence said.

"You never know." Ettie ladled the soup into three bowls and when all of them were seated with soup in front of them, they closed their eyes and said a prayer of thanks for the food. "Bread, anyone?"

"*Jah*, please," Florence said.

"I'll cut it." Elsa-May grabbed the breadknife before Ettie reached it. "You always cut the bread crooked."

Ettie scowled at her oldest sister. "I do not."

71

"You do."

Florence laughed. "I don't know how you two have managed to live together for all this time."

"Why do you say that?" Elsa-May asked in her oldest-sister tone.

"Every time I come here there's an awful lot of arguing."

"There's no arguing," Elsa-May said. "Not when I'm always right."

Ettie giggled. "I don't know what to say about that."

Florence said, "I think maybe you should just keep quiet, Ettie."

"*Jah*, that's what I've found is usually best."

Elsa-May finished cutting the bread and held up a perfectly even slice. "See? It's the same on all sides." She slowly turned the piece of bread from side to side.

"*Wunderbaar*," Ettie said sarcastically.

Florence laughed. "You can cut the bread any time you're at my place, Elsa-May."

"Would you like a piece of bread, Ettie?" Elsa-May asked.

"*Jah*, please. If you can replicate that perfection."

Florence laughed again.

"No problem." Elsa-May turned her attention to cutting the bread and then handed Ettie another perfectly cut slice.

"*Denke*," Ettie said with a nod.

"Where were we up to with things?" Florence asked.

"We were saying you'll find out tomorrow whether John's inherited his father's orchard. Kelly would now know about the story of the missing money and about Levi complaining that the nurse had taken his money," Ettie said.

Elsa-May buttered her bread.

Ettie stared at the thick layer of butter on Elsa-May's bread. "Not too much butter. Remember what the doctor said?"

"Humph. Are you still convinced Levi was killed, Florence?"

"If you had been there too, you would've seen him most insistent that someone was trying to kill him and his death wouldn't be an accident. He told me that about three times."

"That's right, I remember now. He told you it would be the man next door, his son, the nurse, and I think you mentioned one more person."

Ettie placed her soupspoon down and stared at Florence. "Who?"

"I can't remember, but it'll come to me."

"He actually thought his son might try to kill him?" Elsa-May asked.

"I know it's surprising, but that's what he said. I remember now. It was Tony Troyer. Remember? I had you put him on that list. Many years ago, they had plans of going into business together. Levi said something about Tony not being able to raise all the money, so their partnership didn't go ahead."

Elsa-May asked, "Was Tony Troyer at the funeral?"

Ettie shook her head. "He wasn't. There weren't many people there and that's how I remember he definitely wasn't there."

Florence said, "Ettie, perhaps we should pay Tony a visit?"

"What reason will we give for being there?"

"I'm not sure. We'll think of something before we get there."

"We'll do it another time, perhaps in a few days. There are other things that need looking at first," Ettie said. "Like seeing who the real beneficiary of the will is. If Levi was murdered that might give us a good clue where to look for his killer."

"Okay. Good idea." Florence placed another spoonful of soup into her mouth.

"It's good soup, Ettie," Elsa-May said.

"*Denke.*" Ettie could scarcely believe her ears. A positive comment from her older sister was rare indeed.

Elsa-May screwed up her nose, and added, "It just needs a little more salt."

Ettie's elation was short-lived, and she pushed the salt-shaker toward Elsa-May.

CHAPTER 12

*E*ttie looked at the clock on the wall. "It's noon, twelve o'clock," she announced to Elsa-May. It had been raining on and off all day and Elsa-May hadn't even been able to take Snowy for his regular morning walk. "The reading of the will was early this morning. Do you think we should go to John's and see what happened?"

"John's *haus*?"

"That's right."

"If he didn't inherit the farm, he won't be in the mood for visitors."

"Then we won't stay," Ettie said.

"It's not the best day for an outing."

"We can't let the weather hold us back. Besides, I like the rain sometimes."

"*Jah*, when you're indoors."

Ettie chuckled. "Where is your adventurous spirit?"

"It went away when I reached fifty-two, six-months, and two days."

"Okay, I'll go by myself then." Ettie pushed herself to her feet.

Elsa-May had just finished a row and she dropped the knitting into her lap. "Wait up."

"Are you coming with me?"

"I might as well." Snowy looked up and ran to her. "I'm sorry, boy. Perhaps we can go for a walk this afternoon in between rain showers? You go back to your bed and I'll get you a treat." Snowy's ears pricked up on hearing the word 'treat.'

Ettie laughed. "He knows the word, but he's got no intention of going back to his bed until he sees it."

Elsa-May headed to the kitchen with Snowy following close behind. As soon as he was given his treat in the kitchen, he scurried back to his dog bed in the corner to eat it.

"He's happy now," Ettie said as she pulled on her black over-bonnet and picked up her shawl.

"I hope we don't catch a cold in this weather. I've already not been feeling well."

"Stay home then. I'm not forcing you to come with me."

"*Nee*, you're not forcing me, but you have a way of making me do things."

Ettie passed Elsa-May her shawl and bonnet. "These will keep out the rain."

"It's uncomfortable visiting John with how rude Connie is. Is that true, what you told me about what she said to you and Florence?"

"*Jah*, it's true. I didn't know what to say when she asked Florence and me what business was it of ours. Florence should've said we're trying to get to the bottom of who murdered her father-in-law, that's what she should've said. Anyway, we can't let Connie bother us or stand in our way," Ettie said. "Just ignore her if she's rude."

WHEN THEY STEPPED outside to call a taxi, the rain stopped.

Ettie dug Elsa-May with her elbow. "Look there, it's a slice of sunshine in the sky between the clouds. That means it's not going to rain all day, anyway."

"Let's hurry, then, before the rain starts again."

Ettie and Elsa-May had the taxi take them close to the cottage at the apple orchard. As soon as they got out of the taxi, they saw a woman near the front door.

When they walked closer, the woman spoke. "Hello. Are you relatives of Levi's?"

"No, we're friends. We stopped by to see his son, John."

"Oh, nobody's at home. I just knocked. His son is staying here, then?"

"That's right. If you don't mind me asking, how did you know Levi?" Elsa-May asked.

"I was his nurse. I came to the house a few times to look after him when he had a bad leg."

Ettie figured that if the nurse was here, Kelly most likely hadn't caught up with her about the missing money. Now they had the perfect opportunity to ask her some questions.

"I would've gone to his funeral, but I only just found out that he died."

Ettie and Elsa-May introduced themselves and found out that the woman's name was Nella Bridges.

"Why did Levi need a nurse if you don't mind me asking?"

"I don't mind at all. He had quite a few health problems and there was a time there that he could barely look after himself. When he couldn't make it into the clinic, I'd stop by and check on him."

"What were these health problems?"

"He had diabetes, a bad case of reoccurring gout, and heart problems. I heard that he died of heart problems."

"That's what we heard, too," Elsa-May said.

Ettie asked, "Did you ever bring him cookies? Or leave them on his doorstep?"

"No. I would never give him cookies. I always encourage my patients to eat healthy." She shrugged her shoulders. "He was particularly fussy with what he ate because he was—"

"Has a detective been in touch with you yet?" Elsa-May interrupted.

Ettie had been wondering whether she should bring up the issue of the stolen money and Elsa-May had gotten in first.

Nella raised her eyebrows. "No. What detective?"

"It seems that Levi complained to his son about some money missing and he thought you took it. Not knowing how much money was involved, John dismissed it, but then we found the money could have been possibly eight dollars."

"No, eighty thousand dollars, Elsa-May."

"That's what I meant. Eighty thousand dollars."

Nella gasped and put her hand to her chest. "No one thinks I took it, do they?"

"That's what we're saying. I'm sorry to tell you, but you should know that we think Levi might have, because he complained to his son and said you took some money."

Elsa-May added, "And when his son found out there was eighty thousand dollars missing, he had to go to the police. You see, it wasn't really Levi's money and now John might possibly have to pay it back, and he can't with it gone missing."

"Oh, this is dreadful. I'll go to the police right now to clear this whole thing up."

"That might be a good idea," Elsa-May said. "Ask for Detective Kelly; he's handling the case."

Nella stopped, looked back, and then said, "Okay. Thank you."

They stood and watched Nella get into the passenger seat of a white car. Then it zoomed away. Ettie noticed a man was driving and he had black shoulder-length hair and his head nearly reached the roof of the car.

"You could've broken it to her more gently, Ettie."

"You were the one who asked if the detective had been in touch."

Elsa-May pushed out her lips. "I didn't know how else to say it. I feel dreadful for her, but it's best that she know."

"I suppose she would've had a worse shock if the police had found her, and spoke to her first."

"True."

"What do you make of her reaction?" Ettie asked.

"She seemed upset and shocked."

"You think she's innocent?" Ettie asked.

Elsa-May shrugged her shoulders. "I don't know; it's hard to say. She seemed genuinely shocked. And if she had stolen all that money, why would she come back here at all? I mean, you wouldn't, would you?"

"*Nee.* If I was dishonest and had gotten away with something, I'd keep going and not look back."

"Exactly." Elsa-May gave a sharp nod of her head.

As the sisters stood on the porch talking about Nella Bridges, they were distracted by John's red car approaching the house.

Ettie stepped to the edge of the porch. "This is John now."

"I do hope it's been good news for him."

"If not, he won't be happy." Ettie shook her head, thinking about how John's wife would react to hearing they'd been left out of the will.

"And if that's the case, we're not sticking around," Elsa-May said.

"Agreed." Ettie nodded while squinting to see John's face for a clue as to the outcome.

Then she saw his beaming smile, and she knew he'd inherited the orchard. Connie was also smiling.

John got out of the car, gave them a wave, and then he and his wife walked to the house.

"Good news?" Ettie called out.

"Yes, I was left everything."

"Of course, that's what we expected," Connie added.

"I'm sorry, did we make arrangements to meet you ladies here? So much has been happening and we've had so many things on—"

Ettie said, "Do you remember my sister, Elsa-May Lutz?"

"Yes, hello."

After Elsa-May was introduced to Connie, Ettie continued, "I hope you don't mind us being here. We just thought we'd see how things went for you."

"That's nice of you," John said.

Ettie wondered whether they should keep quiet about the nurse, but then saw no real reason not to mention that she'd been there. "Your father's nurse was just here. You would've passed her in the street just now."

"Are you sure it was her?" John asked.

"Yes, it seems the police haven't spoken to her about the missing money yet. She only just learned of Levi's passing and came to pay her respects. She thought you might be here at the house."

"It's a little late for that," Connie said as she stepped onto the porch.

John caught up with his wife and took a bunch of keys out of his pocket. "Don't be like that; we don't know for sure that she was the one who took the money. I'm also not totally convinced that the money ever existed in the first place. All we've got for proof is a receipt with my father's signature, and that could have been forged." He looked at Ettie. "I told the police all that."

Connie turned up her nose. "I doubt anyone would fake a signature."

"We won't keep you," Ettie said. "Do you mind if we use your phone to call for a taxi?"

"By all means, go ahead. On second thought, I could drive you wherever you—"

"No, John! We've got too much to do in the house." Connie looked at the elderly sisters and then stared at her husband. "We've got to get rid of all your father's junk."

"We understand," Elsa-May said. "When someone dies, it creates a lot of work for those left behind."

"We do have to leave for another appointment soon, too," Connie said, staring at one sister and then the other.

"Sorry to interrupt you," Elsa-May said.

Ettie looked at her sister. "You call the taxi, Elsa-May."

While Elsa-May headed to the phone located outside of the cottage, Ettie thought she would do some more questioning. "What do you plan to do with the orchard, John?

"Sell, of course," Connie said before he could answer.

John was just putting a key in the lock when he turned and faced his wife. "We haven't discussed it yet, Connie."

"Why would you keep it? We know nothing about farming."

"It's not exactly farming."

"It's close enough. This isn't the life for me, and you know nothing about it. It's insanity to even consider keeping it."

"We'll have the accountant go over the figures before we decide."

"No!"

"We can talk about this later, Connie."

"There's absolutely nothing to talk about."

Ettie backed away, not wanting to get in the middle of an argument. "I'll see how Elsa-May's getting along with that taxi."

John looked at Ettie. "Thanks for stopping by. I'll call the detective again about that nurse and see where things are up to. I had hoped he would've talked to her by now."

Once John unlocked the door, Connie pushed her way through, ignoring him and Ettie.

"Bye," Ettie said to John as he stood staring at his wife.

Turning his head to look at Ettie, he said, "Yes, goodbye, Ettie, and please say goodbye to your sister for us."

"I will."

Ettie joined Elsa-May at the phone and then together they headed down to the road to wait for the taxi. Just when the taxi came into view, the rain came down again.

Once they were in the back seat, Ettie said, "One thing that puzzles me is this: who left those cookies for Levi?"

"We never found that out, did we?"

"*Nee*, we didn't."

"Let's stop by Florence's *haus* and see if we can find out more about the cookies."

Elsa-May leaned over and told the taxi driver to disregard the original address he was given and she gave him Florence's address.

CHAPTER 13

*O*nce they were seated around Florence's kitchen table, they first told her the news that John had inherited the orchard.

"I'm so glad. Otherwise, John would've been very upset."

"Not to mention Connie," Ettie said with a giggle.

"Now he's got more money to gamble with," Elsa-May said matter-of-factly. "To think Levi worked so hard and was so mean with people, and for what? Now his son is going to fritter it all away."

"I don't know if he will," Ettie said.

"It's very hard for someone to stop gambling when they have a problem, Ettie."

"I think he wanted to keep the orchard. There's another thing we have to tell you, Florence."

Florence opened her eyes wide. "Go on."

"We got to the house before them—before John and Connie—and the nurse was at the house."

"Levi's nurse?"

"*Jah*, she said she'd only just heard about his death and she was there to pay her respects to his relatives."

"What if she'd gone back to the house to get rid of evidence?" Florence asked.

Ettie and Elsa-May looked at each other.

"We hadn't even thought of that," Elsa-May said.

"We mentioned the missing money and asked whether the police had talked to her and she said that they hadn't."

Elsa-May added, "And then she got very distressed and said she was going to the police station to clear the matter up. That's what she told us."

Florence nodded. "It'll be interesting to find out if she ever went there."

"You don't trust her at all, do you?" Ettie asked.

"Levi didn't trust her. He said all along she was the one who took his money. But no one listened to him just like no one listened to me about him being murdered."

Ettie sighed. The whole thing was a puzzle.

Elsa-May leaned toward Florence. "Ettie and I were talking about the cookies. Who do you think would've left him cookies, since no one liked him?"

"*Jah*, that is an interesting question. I've got no idea. I'm sorry I can't help you there."

"You told us he got them out of a package. What did the package look like?"

As Florence thought, her gaze traveled to the ceiling. "A box, I think, maybe with a lid. Red. The wrapping he removed was red, and so was the box. Levi would've mentioned if there was a note with the cookies, and he said he didn't know who left them."

"Do you think they were homemade or store-bought?" Ettie asked.

"I don't think so."

"Which one?" Elsa-May asked.

"I don't know either way. They looked homemade, but it's hard to say these days because some store-bought cookies can look home baked. The package looked like something from a store. I didn't taste them, either. I was afraid to. Levi thought they were good."

Ettie said to Elsa May, "How would we go about finding out who left the cookies there?"

"Ask around, I suppose," she replied.

"But there was no poison in the cookies, so how would that help us?" Florence asked.

Ettie shook her head. "We don't know yet. But sometimes if we can put small pieces in the puzzle they all join and eventually fit together to tell a story."

"Who knows?" Elsa-May said. "Knowing who left the cookies there on that day might give us a lot more information."

"We'll leave you to ask around about the cookies while Elsa-May and I go to the police station to see what's happening with the nurse."

Florence giggled. "I think I've got the easier of the two jobs."

Ettie nodded. "You have."

LATER THAT DAY, Ettie and Elsa-May walked into the police station. They happened to see Kelly talking to the officer at the front desk.

The detective didn't look happy to see them. He motioned for them to move to the other side of the room where they wouldn't be overheard. "Have you heard?" Kelly asked them.

"Heard what?" Elsa-May asked.

"Levi's body is being exhumed. Isn't that why you're here?"

"Why are you doing that?" Ettie asked.

He looked shocked that she would ask that question. And

then one side of his mouth turned upward to form a crooked smile. "We have reason to believe he might've fallen victim to someone who could possibly be a serial killer."

"Really?"

He raised his eyebrows.

"The nurse?" Ettie asked, clutching at her throat.

"I can't say any more than what I've already said."

Elsa-May said, "Because if it's the nurse ... What was her name again, Ettie?"

"Nella Bridges."

"That's right, if it's Nella Bridges, we've only just talked to her."

That got Detective Kelly's attention. "Where was she?"

"At Levi's house," Ettie said.

Elsa-May added, "She said she was there to pay her respects."

Ettie said, "We told her about the missing money, and she didn't know anything about it. She was visibly disturbed and then she said she was coming to the police station to clear it all up with you. Elsa-May told her to ask for you."

"She hasn't been here and we're looking for her. How long ago did you see her?"

"It would've been about two hours ago," Ettie said.

"Was she driving a vehicle?"

Ettie nodded. "A small white car. Actually, she was the passenger."

"Hmm. I don't suppose you know the make and the model?"

Ettie and Elsa-May shook their heads. "But the driver was a tall man with long dark hair."

"If you'll excuse me, ladies, I've got things to do."

"When is his body being exhumed?" Elsa-May asked as he was trying to get them out the door.

"Soon, most likely today or tomorrow. And hopefully, it's a better day than today."

"Before we go, we've just got one quick question and it's the reason we came to see you."

He sighed. "What is it?"

"What happened to the cookies?"

"And what about the container they came in?" Elsa-May added.

Ettie nodded. "Yes, the box too."

"They're still in evidence."

"Can we see them?"

"No!"

Elsa-May frowned at him. "Can you describe the box or package at least? You might have found it in the trash. Not you personally, but the evidence technicians."

"Can't you ask your sister these questions? Mrs. Lapp might have seen all that."

"We did, but she can't remember exactly," Elsa-May said.

"Very well, when I'm not so busy, I'll take a look at the evidence and get back to you with a full description. Will that make you happy?"

"It will. Thank you."

"Can I go now?" he asked.

"Yes," Ettie muttered as she turned around.

Elsa-May and Ettie turned and headed out of the police station.

When they were on the sidewalk, Ettie suggested to Elsa-May, "Maybe it was Nella who brought him those cookies after all."

"But what is …" Elsa-May sighed. "They said there was nothing in the cookies. So, does that mean they were wrong? Or did she kill him in some other way?"

"If she killed him, she's done it in some way that went undetected and made it look like a heart attack. Now, Kelly must be on to something. If the nurse is a serial killer that means she's killed people before so they must know how it was done. Perhaps she used a poison that's not generally tested for in a normal autopsy."

"You might be right. What do we do now?" Elsa-May asked. "Do we go back and tell Florence, so she doesn't have to ask about those cookies now?"

Ettie shook her head. "That sounds like a lot of rushing around and besides, Florence might find something out. Meanwhile, why don't we go to our favorite café?"

Elsa-May raised her eyebrows. "That sounds like the best idea you've had for a while, Ettie."

Ettie giggled. "We can put all our troubles aside for half an hour while we enjoy a piece of cake. Cake that we didn't have to bake."

Arm-in-arm, Ettie and Elsa-May headed up the road toward the café.

"This time, we'll have different cakes and then we'll share."

"Okay," Ettie agreed. They didn't eat out very often, and when they did, they enjoyed it.

CHAPTER 14

*E*ttie and Elsa-May heard nothing else that day about the nurse, but the very next afternoon, Florence knocked on their door.

Ettie opened the door to Florence. "What is it?"

"Do you have news?" Elsa-May asked.

"Yes and no."

"Come in out of the cold." Ettie pulled her into the house by her sleeve.

"I spoke to Dianne Yoder and she said she saw someone at Levi's house the morning he died." Florence sat on the couch and Ettie sat down next to her.

Elsa-May sat on her usual chair. "Firstly, before we go any further we should tell you what we found out from Kelly yesterday."

"The police are exhuming Levi's body," Ettie said.

"They're finally taking me seriously. Good!"

"He wouldn't tell us everything; all he told us was that Levi might've been killed by a serial killer."

Florence gasped. "That's terrible."

"Anyway, I interrupted you. Who did Diane Yoder see?" Elsa-May asked.

"I've come over all trembling. Just give me a moment."

"Would you like a glass of water?" Ettie asked.

"*Jah, denke,* Ettie."

Ettie hurried to the kitchen to get her sister a glass of water. Finally, they might be closer to knowing who killed Levi.

After Florence had swallowed a mouthful of water, she held the glass in her lap and Ettie sat down again.

"Diane Yoder said it was a woman. She saw a woman walking to Levi's house with something in her hands. It was in the early hours of the morning—just on dawn. She said the woman was holding something red."

"It must've been the nurse she saw," Elsa-May said.

"Not necessarily," Ettie said. "What else did Dianne say?"

"Just that she saw a person—a woman—and she thought it odd since Levi hardly got any visitors. That's why she took particular notice."

"What was this woman wearing?"

"I asked her that and Dianne said she doesn't remember."

"She can't have taken too much notice, then," Elsa-May said.

"Dianne did say the woman wasn't Amish. She was an *Englischer.*"

"That narrows it down," Elsa-May said sarcastically. "We're no further ahead. We already know someone left cookies there and we still don't know who it was. I would've guessed that it was a woman rather than a man. Leaving cookies at someone's door is the kind of thing that a woman would do."

Ettie said, "*Jah,* but now we know it was an *Englischer.* That's something we didn't know before."

"Would it help if Dianne saw a red car parked down the road?" Florence asked, blinking rapidly.

"A red car!" Ettie and Elsa-May blurted simultaneously.

"*Jah.*" Florence nodded.

"Ettie, doesn't John have a red car?"

"*Jah*, he does."

"Exactly," Florence said.

"Why didn't you start with the red car?" Elsa-May frowned sternly at Florence while Florence put her hand over her mouth and chuckled.

"Let's think about this carefully," Ettie said. "If it was Connie taking the cookies to Levi's, why would she have done it?"

"And don't they live some distance away?" Elsa-May asked.

"They live a six-hour drive away. I know that John is often away on business trips. I think that's why it took them so long to get here after Levi died, because John had to come back from a business trip before they drove here. What if, when he was away on that business trip, Connie drove here and left the cookies?" Florence asked.

"For what purpose, though? She doesn't strike me as the type of person to do anything nice for anyone and not take credit for it. So, if the cookies didn't kill him and they had no poison in them, should we be bothered about the cookies at all? If Kelly's right about the nurse then we don't have to look any further about the cookies, do we?" Elsa-May asked.

"I think we need to look at the whole picture. The nurse has a white car, if the car we saw her in was hers, so we could probably rule her out for bringing the cookies," Ettie said.

"I don't know why you're still fixated on the cookies!" Elsa-May stared at Ettie.

"It's just that it doesn't add up, that's all. It's not as though I'm worried about the cookies. Well, maybe I am, because it bothers me that someone would leave cookies for him when no one likes him."

"Let it go, Ettie. Anyone could've given him cookies. Anyone at all. If Detective Kelly is exhuming the body, that means he's pretty close to an arrest."

"I've got chills." Florence said.

Ettie said, "Sit closer to the fire."

"Not those sort of chills. Chills about the nurse being a serial killer. What else did the detective say?"

"Nothing much. But the nurse said she was going to the police station to set them straight when we told her that Levi thought she'd taken money, but she didn't show."

"You think she could've killed him for the money?" Florence asked.

"I suppose it's possible," Ettie said.

"Don't serial killers do it because they like to? I suppose if she was going to kill him anyway and she knew he had eighty thousand dollars lying around, maybe she thought she might as well take it."

"We're forgetting about the neighbor in all of this," Ettie said.

"Eric?"

"*Jah*, it seems odd that he would give someone eighty thousand dollars as a gesture of good will, or as a deposit without having any contract or paperwork signed. He did have the receipt signed, but Eric or someone else might have known how Levi signed his name."

"Florence, perhaps you should pay another visit to John and Connie."

Florence stared at Ettie. "And why is that?"

"Because if there was never any eighty thousand, the neighbor's done that for a reason. He might have done it to get money from John, or a huge discount off the purchase price of the orchard."

Florence slowly nodded. "That makes perfect sense. But I'm not going there alone. One of you will have to come with me."

Elsa-May sank down into her chair. "I'm starting to feel that cold coming back."

Ettie rolled her eyes. "I suppose that only leaves me—again. Can we do that tomorrow, Florence? It's too late in the day." Ettie secretly hoped that Detective Kelly would find it in his heart to stop by and tell them about the new autopsy results. If they had exhumed Levi's body that day then surely they would know something tomorrow by the very latest.

"*Jah*, I'm a little too tired to do anything else today. Why don't I collect you tomorrow around mid-morning, Ettie?"

"I'll be waiting."

CHAPTER 15

*W*hen Florence and Ettie drove up to John's house the next morning, Ettie saw a police car there.

"Keep driving," Ettie said.

"I wonder what happened."

"They'd be telling John the results of the new autopsy."

"I wish we knew too." Florence guided her horse and buggy past Levi's cottage.

"We'll have to wait and see. You said there were four people that Levi mentioned who might have killed him?"

"That's right. Eric from next door, John, the nurse, or—"

"Tony Troyer," Ettie said.

"That's right, Tony Troyer."

"Why don't we pay him a visit while we're filling in time? We can come back to Levi's *haus* soon and hope John will tell us what happened."

"You mean John's *haus*."

"*Jah*, I suppose it's his now."

"Tony only lives fifteen-minutes up this road. He wasn't at the funeral," Florence commented.

"Not many people were."

Florence chuckled. "I always told Levi to be nicer to people."

"He was set in his ways, I suppose. I wonder if he made a good profit from his apples. I think he might have and that's why John wanted to keep the orchard."

"I don't know. With Levi, it was hard to tell. I think he saved money by being mean and cutting corners wherever he could."

"I hope Tony's at home."

"What does he do with himself nowadays?" Florence asked Ettie.

"He'd be most likely retired by now. Last I heard of him, he was doing odd jobs here and there, filling in for workers when they were sick or had time off."

When Florence turned the buggy up the narrow lane that led to Tony's house, they saw him sitting on his porch. When they got closer, he stood and his large red dog made his way toward the buggy.

"Rusty, come back. Heel!"

The dog stopped, turned slowly, and went back to Tony. "I'm sorry about that. I'll put him inside." He grabbed the dog and pushed him into the house. "He's not much of a watch-dog. He likes people too much." He moved toward them. "How are you ladies today?"

Ettie and Florence stepped down from the buggy.

"How are you, Tony?" Florence asked.

"*Jah*, I'm good, and how are you two ladies?"

"Good," Ettie said.

"Have you recovered from what happened the other day, Florence?"

"With Levi?"

"*Jah*."

"Sort of."

"It was a dreadful shock for her," Ettie said. "Very traumatic."

"I had intended to go to Levi's funeral, but something came up at the last minute and I wasn't able to go. I know he was a particular friend of yours, Florence."

"I suppose he was in a way. Do you mind if we ask you a couple of questions about Levi and his orchard?"

"Of course, I don't mind. We can sit on the porch rather than go inside and be licked by the dog. Rusty's a little too friendly. He'd jump all over you and lick you to death if he could."

Ettie laughed. "The porch is fine."

Once they were all seated, Florence said, "It's about Levi."

Tony nodded. "Did he say I owed him money, or something?"

"*Nee*, not at all."

"Well, I don't. I thought it might be something he'd do—to take a last parting jab at me."

Florence cleared her throat. "It was nothing like that. That's not why we're here. We're hoping you might be able to give us some information. He predicted his own death, in a way. I don't know if you know this, but I was the last person to speak with him before he died."

He nodded sympathetically. "I know."

"He told me that if he died and it looked like an accident, it wouldn't be. He said someone was out to kill him."

Tony leaned back. "He didn't say that I was going to kill him, did he?"

"Not in so many words." Ettie didn't want to reveal too much. "Did you have any recent dealings with Levi?"

"I hadn't talked to him in years. Ever since we were going into partnership and he changed his mind."

"He did?"

"*Jah*, he did. I'd nod to him whenever I saw him and that was it. He went back on his word and I've got no time for anyone who does that."

Ettie said, "I might as well tell you that you were one of the people Levi named who wanted him dead."

Tony frowned and then spluttered, "You're joking, aren't you?"

Ettie shook her head. "I'm afraid not."

"It's true," Florence said. "He told me himself."

"Who were the other people?"

Florence shook her head. "I'd rather not say."

"I knew he'd do something like this. That's just the way he was. I don't know why he didn't like me. If I did anything to upset him, I've got no idea what it was."

Ettie tried her best to figure things out. "When you two had the idea of going into business together, that was many years ago, wasn't it?"

"That's right, and like I said, I've had nothing to do with him since. I can't believe he'd think I'd kill him."

Ettie figured that part was true because Florence always said he had few friends and she thought no one visited him. "If you can think of a reason why he said that, will you let us know?"

"I will. Is that why you stopped by?" Tony asked.

Florence nodded. "*Jah*, we're trying to find out who killed him."

"Florence believes he was killed, and it wasn't just a heart attack."

"I hope you find your answers." The dog barked from inside the house and then they heard scratching sounds. "Stop it!" Tony yelled out. Then there was silence.

"*Denke*," Ettie said as she rose to her feet.

As they got into the buggy, Tony called out, "Don't be surprised if you never find an answer. A lot of things Lousy Levi did and said never made sense."

Florence smiled and gave him a wave before turning her horse to face the road.

CHAPTER 16

*E*ttie was tired, so instead of going anywhere else Florence took Ettie home. She hadn't been home long when Detective Kelly knocked on her door. It was just she and Elsa-May at home.

"Can I come inside?" He looked a little sheepish.

"Certainly."

When he sat down on one of the wooden chairs in the living room, Ettie asked, "How did the second autopsy and the exhuming of the body—?"

Elsa-May interrupted before Ettie could finish her sentence. "It's called an exhumation, Ettie."

Ettie ignored her sister and continued to wait for an answer from the detective.

"That's why I'm here. I didn't exactly tell you ladies the whole story."

Ettie leaned forward. "What did you leave out?"

"There was no court-ordered exhumation. Instead, the truth was that I got a tip-off that Levi's son was exhuming his father's body for cremation."

"What? You lied to us?" Ettie was puzzled and then remembered the odd look of amusement on his face when he'd lied to them.

"I'm sorry. It was wrong of me."

Ettie shook her head. "It certainly was. All this time we thought that poor nurse might be responsible for Levi's death."

Kelly's lips turned down at the corners. "All this time? I believe I only told you that yesterday. And, I am sorry."

"Now tell me again. John exhumed his father's body of his own accord?" Ettie asked.

"That's right."

"I don't think it's right for a man in your position to tell such outrageous untruths. If we had told anyone and word got around that the poor lady was a serial killer that could have been devastating to her, especially in her position."

He put a hand on his dark grey suit, in the position of his heart. "I swear to you ladies I will not do anything like that again. I am sorry. I let you think the department was exhuming his body and then as an error in judgment, I added the rest. Am I forgiven?"

Ettie slowly nodded and Elsa-May said, "I suppose we'll have to forgive you. John never mentioned to us that he was thinking of doing anything of the kind."

"It doesn't make sense," Ettie said.

"I was too late, I'm afraid. The body was gone when I got to the crematorium. By the time the call came into the station, there was no time to get a court order to stop the cremation."

"Why would John do that?" Elsa-May asked.

"When I asked him that very same question, he said he remembered that's what his father had wanted. I must say I gave little credence to what your sister said about Levi being murdered until I heard John Hochstetler was cremating his father's body. You two know why people are often anxious to do that, don't you?"

"Yes, of course. It's to hide evidence of a murder."

Elsa-May nodded. "Yes. Evidence that was missed on the initial autopsy."

Ettie knew Levi wouldn't have wanted to be cremated. It wasn't the Amish way.

The detective looked at Ettie. "What are you thinking, Mrs. Smith? You've been very quiet."

"I've got a few things running through my mind. I don't think John's telling the truth about what Levi wanted."

"That's what I suspected. I've been to a handful of Amish funerals, and have never been to a cremation. He's trying to keep something hidden."

"Have you questioned John again—I mean more thoroughly?"

"We've talked to him but not questioned him too much about it. We will and we're still looking for Nella Bridges. She's done a decent job of disappearing into thin air."

"Perhaps she heard that someone thought she was a serial killer," Elsa-May commented.

Detective Kelly wagged his finger at Elsa-May. "Forgiven, but not forgotten?"

"Perhaps as punishment someone could go over the autopsy results very carefully again?" Elsa-May asked.

"That's taking place as we speak."

Ettie said, "I still can't believe you told us the serial killer thing. It's most unprofessional"

"I'm sorry, again, that I told you that. I needed to keep a clear head and I told you the first thing that came to me. It was just off the top of my head."

Elsa-May gasped. "Perhaps you need a vacation if the job is getting to you?"

"I couldn't tell you what was really happening when you

came into the station, and I was in a rush. While I was speaking to you, one of my men was tracking down which crematorium Levi was being taken to. To put it frankly, I was just trying to get rid of you and put you off the track so you'd keep right out of my way. I didn't want you finding John and telling him anything."

"Who gave you the tip-off that John intended to cremate his father?" Ettie asked

"It was an anonymous call into the station."

"Man or woman?" Elsa-May asked.

Kelly folded his arms over his chest. "I'm afraid I can't give out that information. I continually bend the rules for you ladies, but there are some things I just can't tell you."

"And what do you know about Nella Bridges?" Ettie asked, knowing he wouldn't tell her that either.

"All I can say is we're looking for her. If you see her or hear from her, be sure to let me know. Tell her to call into the station."

Ettie nodded. "We will, but we're not expecting to see her."

He shook his head. "Even her brother didn't know where she was."

The phone buzzed and Kelly answered it. "I'll be one minute." He stepped outside, not noticing his notebook as it fell onto the floor.

Ettie leaned forward to pick it up and as she did she read what was on the page that it had opened to. "Elsa-May, this must be Nella's brother's business. Bridges Roofing."

"I've seen that sign before. I know where it is."

Ettie put the book back on the chair, and the moment she was back in her seat, Kelly returned. "I'll have to go," he said as he grabbed the notebook and slipped it into his pocket.

"Do you have time for tea or coffee?" Ettie asked.

"And cake?" Elsa-May added.

"Some other time. I've got another appointment to make." The detective left just as quickly as he'd arrived.

CHAPTER 17

When Ettie sat back down on her couch, she heaved a large sigh. "Oh, dear. It's hard to believe John would've done that to his father's body. He told no one, I'm certain of it. He knew Florence was close to his father and he didn't even tell her."

"Kelly is right; it makes him look really guilty. He had to know that the autopsy missed something. Or hadn't tested for a certain kind of poison maybe."

"It seems the most likely reason for a sudden cremation. Levi had only been in the ground a few days." Ettie shook her head while thinking of Levi. He certainly wouldn't have wanted to be cremated.

Elsa-May made clicking noises with her tongue. "I can't believe Kelly lied to us."

"I know. It was most unexpected with him being in law enforcement. I wouldn't have thought he'd do that."

"He's got no respect for us, Ettie."

"Is that what it is?"

"What else could it be?"

"He said he couldn't tell us what was happening at the time. Maybe he knew we'd ask too many questions, or he might have thought we'd get in the way."

Elsa-May shook her head. "It's just not right. He didn't have to lie."

"You're right about that," Ettie said.

"What? I'm right about it not being right?"

"*Jah.*"

Elsa-May sighed.

"What should we do now?"

"Start cooking dinner."

"*Nee,*" Ettie said.

"Are we going out?"

"*Nee,* we never go out. I meant what are we going to do about John? Should we talk to him again and see why he did what he did?"

"That's a silly idea. If he was covering evidence, do you think he would tell us?"

Ettie blinked rapidly. "I don't think it's silly. We could get an inkling of what he's up to."

"I suppose. Can we do it tomorrow?"

"Okay."

That night, Ettie tossed and turned, unable to sleep. Her mind was roiling like clothes in a washing machine.

There was the early morning sighting of an *Englischer* taking something to Levi's house. The woman—if it had been a woman—would've been the one who'd bought and delivered the cookies. She'd driven a red car, but left it parked on the road, so she could walk to the house undetected and unnoticed by Levi as he slept.

Why had Levi mentioned Tony's name as one of the four potential killers if they'd had no recent dealings?

Had the detective also been lying to them when he indicated that Nella Bridges might have been a serial killer, or was that actually true? Why had Nella disappeared?

Ettie was also disturbed by John's actions in having his father cremated just days after the Amish funeral.

As if all that wasn't enough, there was also the matter of the missing money—if it ever existed at all.

CHAPTER 18

The next morning, Ettie staggered out of bed and sat down at the kitchen table, elbows propped on the table and her head in her hands.

"What happened to you?" Elsa-May asked.

"Coffee, please."

"Coming up." Elsa-May poured the rest of the coffee she'd already made into a small cup. "There you are."

Ettie took a sip. "*Mmm. Denke.* I couldn't sleep. Everything kept tumbling around in my head."

Elsa-May sat down at the table, and together they sat in silence for a few moments.

Finally, Elsa-May broke the silence. "Is John our first stop?"

"I don't know."

"You tell me. What are you thinking?"

"I'd like to find out more from Kelly, but now that he's taken to lying to us we can't trust him."

"Let's bypass him, shall we? I suppose we should tell Florence what we know."

"Later," Ettie said. She took another sip of coffee.

"We won't tell Florence?"

"*Nee*, it won't do any good. We'll tell her when we know more. No need to worry her. She's had a dreadful time, being there when Levi died so suddenly."

"Okay. First stop is John. I'll cook you some eggs."

"*Denke.*"

"Unless you want to go back to bed, Ettie? You look like you could do with more sleep."

"I won't get any sleep until we know what's going on. Everyone looks guilty and if they don't, they look guilty by not appearing guilty."

"You mean Tony?"

"*Jah.*"

"It bothers me that Tony says he's had nothing to do with Levi. He's hiding something, I'm certain of it. But what?"

"If he's got a secret, who would know what it is?"

Ettie drummed her fingers on the table as she thought. "Who are Tony's friends?"

"He was seeing a lot of Maud Fisher. The two of them have been on and off for years."

"Hmmm, I don't know if he'd share secrets with Maud. Who else? No, let's leave him for a moment. We'll put him on the shelf and see if we can find out anything about Nella from her brother. That book of Kelly's might have fallen open on that page for a reason."

"*Jah*, and I know where his workshop is. Why don't we pay him a visit before we visit John?"

"We could. What will we say?" Ettie asked.

Elsa-May cracked two eggs into a bowl. "Weren't we talking about getting a new roof?"

"*Nee*, there's nothing wrong with our roof. We've never thought about a new roof."

"We've talked about it. We're talking about it now. It

wouldn't hurt to say we're thinking about getting the roof looked at or something."

Ettie sighed. "I don't know. I don't like to waste anyone's time. He'll want to come out and look at the roof and measure it, and on and on it will go."

"*Nee*, Ettie. We won't let it get that far. We'll get him talking about Levi and then see what else he says." Elsa-May whisked the eggs.

"Good thinking." When Ettie took another sip of coffee, she noticed that

Elsa-May's lips were turned slightly upward at the corners and she was looking pleased with herself.

ETTIE AND ELSA-MAY got out of the taxi at Bridges Roofing. "You do all the talking then, Elsa-May."

"Let's be realistic. That'll never happen."

"You start off then, because I'm not comfortable telling him we're looking to get a new roof."

"They quote on things all the time. They don't mind."

Ettie bit her tongue. There was no use telling Elsa-May there was nothing wrong with their roof. She knew that very well, but at the same time, she couldn't think of another reason to talk to Nella's brother without being obvious.

They walked into the warehouse and saw workers down at one end.

"That looks like an office there," Ettie said, nudging Elsa-May in that direction.

"Okay. I hope he's here."

"I'm sure he will be."

Before they got there, they heard a man talking on the phone. Elsa-May stuck her head into the office. He quickly ended the call, sprang to his feet and stepped toward them. "Good morning. How can I help you?"

He was tall, with jet-black shoulder-length hair and large bushy eyebrows. When she realized he'd been the man who had driven Nella to Levi's house the other day, Ettie's nerves took over. "We're here about a new roof." Looking straight ahead she ignored Elsa-May's look of disapproval burning through her. She'd told Elsa-May to do all the talking and now she'd gone back on it. Her sister hated it when that happened. Of course, Ettie did, too, when it went the other way around.

"Are you the owner of the business?" Elsa-May asked.

"Yes, I'm Justin Bridges."

"I'm Elsa-May Lutz and this is my sister, Ettie Smith. We're not sure if we need one—a new roof, or not," Elsa-May said. "But we'd like to get an idea of what roofing material is available nowadays."

"Our house is quite old," Ettie added.

"Sure, I can show you some options on the computer. Let's sit at the table."

The three of them sat down at the table and Ettie and Elsa-May sat either side of Justin. He showed them various types of materials and asked them questions about their own roof. After a while he said, "Would you like me to come out and take a look at your roof? You might just need a few repairs. There's no point spending money on a new roof if you don't need one."

"That's exactly what I said." Ettie grinned at Elsa-May.

"We'll just think about it a little longer. We don't want to waste your time," Elsa-May said.

"Would you be Nella's brother?" Ettie asked him. He would've seen them out in front of Levi's house when he'd driven his sister there. Ettie kept quiet about that part, knowing that most *Englischers* thought all Amish women looked the same because they dressed alike.

"I am. Do you know her?"

"We do. She was looking after a very good friend of ours. He just died recently."

"I'm sorry to hear that. Nella would be very upset about that. She takes it very hard when one of her patients dies."

"What a coincidence this is. We were going to call her place of employment today to thank her for looking after him so well. Maybe you could give us her phone number instead?" Elsa-May asked.

"My sister and I don't talk often. I tried to call her yesterday but her phone was disconnected. Is Levi the man who was your friend?"

"Yes." Ettie knew he probably remembered that from the police who came looking for Nella in connection with Levi's death.

He nodded. "If I hear from her, I'll let her know you want to thank her. It'll mean a lot to her."

"Thank you," Elsa-May said.

Ettie shook her head. "It was such a sudden departure."

"I did a quote for him once. What bothers me is that there was some kind of rumor about my sister taking money from Levi."

"We heard that. I wouldn't worry too much about it."

His dark eyebrows drew together. "If you were close with Levi you might know where the rumor started. Was it anything to do with Tony Troyer?"

Ettie gasped. "You know Tony?"

"Tony recommended me to Levi to do some work on his house some time back."

"We didn't know that," Elsa-May said.

Ettie said, "Levi didn't have many friends. I think the closest friend he had was Tony Troyer, but then they had that falling out."

"It wasn't so much of a falling out. Things happen like

that when friends borrow money from each other. Unless there's a firm agreement in place things can go wrong."

"I didn't know Tony had borrowed money from Levi."

Justin shook his head. "It was the other way around. Some time back, Levi was trying to get his son out of financial problems and it nearly sent him broke. He would've gone broke, too, if it wasn't for Tony loaning that money to tide him over until the next selling season."

"How do you know all this?" Ettie asked.

"I've known Tony for years. He used to do insulation and I do roofing."

Elsa-May said, "Tony and Levi were thinking of going into business together many years ago. But the story I heard was that Tony couldn't come up with the full amount of the money at the right time."

"I think what you heard was Levi changing the story, and that way he saved face if anybody had heard about a transaction with money between the two men."

Ettie nodded. "That would make sense."

Justin chuckled. "I only met Levi the once, but I know Tony quite well and he's said some things about Levi. Then my sister took care of him. But all that is nothing to do with roofs."

"No, it's not," Elsa-May said.

"But what I can't understand," Ettie said, "is why Tony was so upset with Levi only very recently."

Justin exhaled heavily and scratched behind his ear. "Let me just say this, when men have a falling out, there's very often a woman who is at the center of their disagreement."

Ettie tried to work out what he was saying. Was a woman stirring up trouble between the two men, or did they both like the same woman? Nella perhaps? Nella was an *Englischer*, she was in her forties, and she was attractive. The two men in their seventies would've found a woman like that extremely attractive. "Are you talking about your sister?"

"I can't say more. I've had the police snooping around. I hope they don't seriously think my sister stole that man's money."

From his twisted smile, Ettie knew she'd hit the nail on the head. Both Levi and Tony liked Nella and that had been the source of their most recent falling out. Tony had chosen not to tell them that part of his history with Levi.

Elsa-May pointed to a roof on the screen. "I like that color roof. What do you call that?"

"That color is called gunmetal gray. It's more of a charcoal."

They'd come there to find something out, and that's exactly what they had done. "We really shouldn't take up any more of your time, Justin."

"I don't mind at all. I'll stop by and have a look at your roof and give you an assessment."

"Maybe some other time. At the moment, we've got more pressing things to do on the place, like bathroom repairs." Elsa-May stood up and so did Ettie.

"It's not leaking at this stage, so there can't be too much wrong with it. Elsa-May tends to worry too much about things. I've always said, if it's not broken, don't fix it." Ettie smiled at Justin.

"You could say that about most things, Mrs. Smith, but with roofs it's different. Your roof could be leaking, and you might not know it. Moisture might have gone through all the timbers, down the sides of your walls and all through the place creating mold, and moisture attracts all manner of pests."

Ettie glared at Elsa-May. She knew this would happen and that's why she didn't want to pretend they were worried about the roof.

"What I'll do is get my grandson to look at the roof. He often stops by. He's a builder. He doesn't do roofs, but he'll know if something's wrong with it. If he finds something wrong with the roof we'll give you a call."

"Very well. If that's what you prefer to do."

"Thanks for your time," Ettie said as she walked toward the door.

"Might we call for a taxi?" Elsa-May asked.

He picked up the phone on his desk. "I'll call one for you."

"It was lovely chatting with you, Justin."

He gave them a smile and a nod.

As soon as they got into the back seat of the taxi, Elsa-May gave the driver John's address, and then turned to her sister. "Ettie, what do you think of that?"

"I think it was a bit lame saying your grandson is a builder and doesn't do roofs. I didn't know where to look. Jeremiah could fix a roof or build a new one. Couldn't any builder do a roof?"

"Ettie! I'm not talking about the roof! I'm talking about what he said about his sister."

"Oh. Do you believe it?"

"I don't know." Elsa-May whispered, "Do you really think that those two men would've been interested in a woman at their age?"

"It makes me shudder thinking about it," Ettie replied.

"And would they really like an *Englischer*? Surely it's only the silly young men who are attracted to outsiders."

Ettie sighed. "I don't think they ever grow up. Men are always boys at heart. They were both men living alone, so why wouldn't they be attracted to an attractive woman? I can understand why Levi was attracted to a pretty nurse who was looking after him, but where would Tony have met her?"

"Bother! We should've asked Justin that."

Ettie patted her sister's hand. "Never mind. We can't go

back and ask him that now. Tony's met her somewhere. Maybe even at Levi's house for all we know. Hang on a minute. Didn't Justin say that he knew Tony and had known him for a while?"

"That's right. You know what, Ettie?"

"What?"

"What if Nella Bridges let Levi know she wasn't interested in him and that's when he made up the allegations about her stealing his money?"

"That would be a dreadful thing for him to do. I don't think even he would go that far and be that awful."

"We're talking about a man with the nickname Lousy Levi."

"If what you say is true, how does that explain the neighbor saying the eighty thousand is missing? And why has Nella Bridges disappeared?" Ettie nibbled on the end of a fingernail. "It seems the more we find out the deeper the mystery becomes."

"You said you didn't believe in coincidences, but we just experienced one. Nella's brother knows Tony Troyer."

"I don't think that's a coincidence. They're both in the building trade. Tony used to install insulation."

"We didn't know that before we went there. We only knew that Justin was Nella's brother."

Ettie shook her head. "It still doesn't make it a coincidence."

Elsa-May pressed her lips firmly together, choosing not to argue the point. "What's our plan next, with John?"

"I'm too stunned about what Justin said just now to think properly."

"The cremation, Ettie."

"*Jah!*" Ettie was reminded that Levi's son had had his father's body exhumed to cremate it just days after his Amish funeral. It was an odd thing to do by anyone's standards.

"Surely he'd know his father wouldn't want cremation. Everyone would find that strange," Elsa-May said.

Ettie raised her eyebrows. "Maybe he didn't care. We'll soon find out. There's something else."

"What?"

"Let me see now." Ettie twisted her prayer *kapp* strings around in her fingers while she thought. "Something else he said."

"Justin?"

"*Jah.* He more or less told us Levi and Tony liked his sister, and then there was something else. It's on the tip of my tongue."

"On the tip of your brain, you mean."

"Bother! I can't think what it is. There was another sliver of information in something he said." Ettie sighed. "I really need to start writing things down as I think of them."

"Don't think about it, and it'll come to you—eventually."

"Okay. I only hope we have that long."

CHAPTER 19

*E*ttie and Elsa-May had just closed the doors after getting out of the taxi at John's house when they heard yelling coming from within the house. They stared at each other, not knowing what to do. Ettie looked around at the taxi, already halfway down the driveway. It was too far away to call it back to make a quick getaway. They were stuck.

"This is awkward," Ettie said.

"Let's walk over to Eric's house and see if we can call a taxi back home from there. I just don't want to be around all that yelling."

"Let's go."

They hadn't taken two steps when they heard someone calling from the front of the house. "Good morning."

They had no choice but to turn around. They saw John looking at them and smiling as if nothing had happened.

"Good morning, John. We just came to visit you, and we didn't see your car anywhere, so we thought you weren't home."

"That's why we didn't knock," added Ettie.

"Please, come in, if you don't mind all the mess. We're sorting through some things."

They walked into the house, to see things all over the floor and things pulled out of cupboards and stacked haphazardly on the countertops.

"We've emptied out every drawer and cabinet trying to find that eighty thousand dollars that my father said was stolen. We got to thinking maybe he had just misplaced it."

"Ettie does things like that all the time," Elsa-May said.

Elsa-May was wrong about that, but Ettie couldn't disagree. The last thing she wanted was to argue after listening to the fight between John and Connie just now.

"We haven't found it yet," Connie snarled.

"Has Eric from next door said anything further about it?" Elsa-May asked.

"He's putting us under a lot of pressure to sell to him, minus his deposit."

"That's why we're looking around for the money," Connie said.

"So, you'd consider selling now?" Ettie asked.

"Yes, we absolutely would. One hundred percent," Connie answered for her husband.

"We'd consider it for the right price, and so far, Eric hasn't come up with a price that we would consider."

Ettie got the idea that Connie would've expected the place to be worth a lot of money. Maybe they even expected twice what the orchard was worth, simply because the man next door wanted it so badly.

They hadn't been asked to take a seat, so Ettie and Elsa-May stood awkwardly watching Connie and John sift through Levi's belongings.

Connie looked up at them. "I suppose you heard about the cremation? Is that why you're here?"

"We heard something about it." Ettie then looked at John,

hoping he'd explain why he had chosen to cremate his father after he'd been buried.

"It was after the funeral that I remembered the conversation my father and I had many years ago. He expressed his wish to be cremated. I only wished that I had remembered that before the burial. But I remembered and was able to fulfill his wish."

"Better late than never," Connie said.

"That's most unusual, for an Amish person to want to be cremated."

"My father thought for himself about things like that."

"He was Amish, and it's not our way," Elsa-May said to John.

When Connie and John looked a little bit shocked at Elsa-May's tone, Ettie knew she'd have to soften her sister's words. "What Elsa-May means is that it's an unusual choice, but not one that would affect him being at home with God."

"That's exactly what he said, Ettie," John said.

"Do you think it was that important to him?" Elsa-May asked.

"It cost me a lot of money to do it, Elsa-May—many thousands of dollars. My father and I hadn't always gotten along. Our relationship was rocky ever since I left the community. This was the last thing I could do for him. If I didn't think it mattered, I wouldn't have done it."

Elsa-May slowly nodded. The way John's eyes were tearing up while speaking about doing the last thing for his father, Ettie figured he must be genuine. Detective Kelly had thought John was hiding evidence by having Levi's body exhumed and cremated. It was a suspicious looking move, but talking to the man in front of her, he just seemed like a son wanting to do this one last thing for his father.

"Yes, I would imagine that would've cost quite a lot of money."

Ettie looked at Connie, wondering if she minded spending that much money on something. And that led Ettie to wonder if John had a gambling problem like they'd heard. Would someone with a gambling problem spend money fulfilling his father's wishes when he could have taken that money and gambled it to feed his addiction? Had they been fighting over the cost of the cremation just now?

"What are your thoughts on the cremation, Connie?" Ettie asked.

"Just another waste of money. John's father is ending up the same place either way whether he's buried or cremated. I don't see the sense in wasting all that money and that's what I told John."

"What's done is done," John said in a rather firm voice.

When John and Connie kept ignoring them and carried on sifting through everything they could find, Ettie and Elsa-May asked to use their phone, then said goodbye and left them to it.

As they walked to the phone, Ettie said, "It's unusual that we haven't heard from Florence."

"We should stop by her place now and tell her all we've learned."

"She won't believe any of it."

CHAPTER 20

*H*alf an hour later, they were sitting down with Florence, sipping hot tea and nibbling cookies.

"I hope these aren't the cookies you got from Levi's house," Elsa-May joked.

"I didn't eat them when he was alive and I certainly wouldn't eat them now. Wherever they are."

"In evidence," Ettie said. "I can't work out whether they've got the stale cookies in evidence, or just the box."

"I suppose it would be the cookies that were in the box," Elsa-May said, "as well as the box and packaging. They might have put the cookies in those zip lock bags they use for evidence."

"Seems weird. I just saw cookies in the box when Levi opened it."

They proceeded to tell Florence everything they knew.

"Levi never mentioned anything to me about wanting to be cremated. It certainly was an unusual choice. I didn't know what he wanted. The only time he ever talked to me about dying was the day that he died. The only thing he was concerned about then was me getting to the bottom of his

125

murder. And I feel I've failed him. I thought the police would listen to me, I really did."

"They listened to you and that's why they ordered an autopsy. If it weren't for you, they would have just thought it was a heart attack and let it go."

"I suppose you're right, but they still haven't found out anything."

"If there's anything to find, Detective Kelly will find it. I know he's suspicious too, but he just won't admit it. That's why he jumped all over the cremation as soon as he got wind of it. He thought there was something suspicious."

"It's not uncommon for them to miss things in autopsies," Elsa-May said. "So I've heard, anyway."

"If there were anything to find out they would've found it by now, I'm sure of that," Florence said. "I still can't figure out what Justin said to you about the two men liking the same woman. Levi and Tony Troyer. I certainly had no idea that Levi had his eyes on anyone."

"We guessed it was his sister that Justin was talking about, but he wouldn't say it."

"What do we do now?" Florence asked her sisters.

Ettie said, "I don't know, but I find it odd that Levi would think his son would try to kill him. Justin said Levi borrowed money from Tony to help John out with his debts and maybe he was charging John interest."

Florence chuckled. "That would be just like him to charge a relative interest. Especially his only son."

"Only child," Elsa-May corrected.

"So, it could be that Levi had borrowed a lot of money to help John, and John had a big debt to his father. Now that his father's gone, that debt has been wiped. Not only that, now John's inherited the orchard."

"We should write all this down, so we don't forget," Florence said.

"Why don't we do just that?" Elsa-May said.

"We'll put it on one of my spare recipe cards." Florence pulled out her recipe box from a drawer, and then took out a pen and an empty recipe card. "John's motive might have been money." She looked at her two sisters. "Then the man next door's motives would be what?"

Elsa-May said, "With Levi out of the way, he might've thought he had a better chance of getting the orchard."

Florence scribbled that on her card. "And then we have the nurse."

"We still don't know the nurse's motive. It doesn't make sense she would kill one of her patients. And now we know Kelly was making that up about the serial killer business. It wasn't very nice of him."

"So we'll put that down as unknown for the nurse's motive, and then we have Tony Troyer, and his possible motive might've been jealousy if the two of them loved the same woman. Maybe she had rejected each of them, and told each that she was interested in the other one."

"You mean she told Tony she was interested in Levi and told Levi she was interested in Tony?"

"That's right." Florence giggled.

"Let's stay on the track with believable scenarios," Elsa-May said, looking annoyed with Florence.

"I just don't see that lovely young woman with either of those men."

"Neither do I, Ettie," Elsa-May said. "Unless it's true that love is blind."

Ettie giggled at what her older sister said. "Blind, and takes away people's common sense also."

"So is that the four people he named taken care of?" Elsa-May asked Florence.

"That's it."

"Let me see that list." Ettie peered at the list. Something

was off. None of these were strong enough motives to kill someone. There had to be something else happening that they still didn't know about.

"What's the matter, Ettie?"

"Just look at the list, Elsa-May. Let's just suppose that Levi was right and someone did kill him, and it was one of these four people. You saw how John was highly emotional about performing his father's last wish. It doesn't seem likely to me that he would be like that after killing his father."

"He could've, Ettie. He could've killed his father and then regretted it deeply. Also, people who habitually lie are often very good at it. They're called psychopaths."

Ettie sighed. Her eldest sister would always disagree with her no matter what, even if she really believed the same as she.

"Then why would two Amish men in their seventies like the same woman who was a good twenty years younger, and an *Englischer* at that? It's not practical that they would pursue an *Englisch* woman—the both of them. And then we have the man next door claiming he paid Levi all that money. It's odd that he's not making much fuss about it. He's never gone to the police about it."

"Levi never went to the police about it either," Florence pointed out.

"I think we can rule the neighbor out. It doesn't make sense to kill Levi in the hope that the person who would inherit the farm might want to sell it to him. And why would a nurse turn around and kill a patient?"

"If she's not guilty, why would she disappear?" Elsa-May asked Ettie.

"I don't know. She could be frightened. She could think that she appears guilty and can't face it, especially since she's been charged once before over something she probably didn't do."

"The trouble with you, Ettie, is that you always think people are innocent."

"That's not correct. I just see both sides of things."

Florence said, "The other thing is that Levi could've been totally wrong. Nobody might have been out to kill him."

"Somehow, I believe him," Ettie said. "I've never been one to believe in coincidences. I believe you were meant to be there that day, and something within Levi made him tell you of his fears right then when he did."

CHAPTER 21

$\mathcal{O}$n their way home, Ettie and Elsa-May stopped at a food store close to their house.

"I feel like something sweet," Elsa-May said.

"What's new?" Ettie replied. "We just want something quick and easy for dinner."

The sisters split up and went to opposite ends of the store. Ettie came across one of the workers she knew stacking the shelves.

"Hello, Mrs. Smith."

"Hello, Bernie. We're just having a quick look for something for dinner. What have you got there?"

Bernie laughed. "These are cookies. They won't be any good, unless you have food allergies and can't have nuts."

"I don't have allergies and neither does my sister." Ettie stared at the cookies. There were chocolate chip and chocolate covered in the same packet. That's how Florence had described the cookies that Levi had been given. "Give me a look at one of those."

Bernie handed the red packet over.

Ettie stared at the package, trying to recall who had said

they'd seen someone carrying something red and walking toward Levi's place. In bold letters, it stated the cookies were gluten free and free of nuts. "Thank you." She handed the package back.

"No good?"

"Do many people buy these?"

"Enough for us to stock them. We had a man who used to come in for them often, but I heard he died."

"Levi Hochstetler?"

"I don't know his name. He was an Amish man, an old Amish man."

"Thank you, Bernie."

"You'd probably know him."

"Yes, I think I do."

Ettie hurried to Elsa-May and pulled on her arm. "What is it, Ettie?"

"I know what happened. I need to call Detective Kelly." Without saying anything further, Ettie headed to the pay phone outside the store. Ettie told Kelly she needed to see him at her house as soon as he could get there. Then Ettie went back inside and encouraged her sister to head home.

"We haven't finished shopping."

"Just grab anything and let's go. I'm fairly certain I know what happened to Levi."

Ettie told Elsa-May she'd called Kelly from the pay phone at the store and asked Kelly to meet them at their house. "I've also called a taxi."

～

WHEN DETECTIVE KELLY got to their home, Ettie led him to the living room. He took a seat and put his hands in his lap. "What is it?"

"The four people Levi mentioned to Florence are innocent. He tried to whisper something to Florence just before he died, but he couldn't talk."

"Who do you think killed him?"

"The nurse's brother, Justin."

The detective's face remained deadpan. "Why would this man have killed Levi?"

"He killed Levi because of his sister. I believe she stole the eighty thousand dollars and Justin had to kill him to stop her from going to jail." Kelly opened his mouth, but Ettie put her hand up. "I'm not finished. At first, Justin made an agreement with Levi that he wouldn't go to the police, and that's why Levi never went to the police about the money. Possibly, Justin told him that he'd try to get the money from her, but wasn't able to because then something changed. Levi felt the financial pressure of his son's money problems with his gambling habit, and then Eric the neighbor was constantly asking for his money back or insisting he sell the orchard to him as per their original agreement."

"You're convinced the nurse's brother killed Levi?"

"Yes."

"How?"

"He was the one who left the cookies at the door."

Kelly's lip curled. "There was no poison in the cookies. I've told you that before."

"No, there wasn't. What was in the cookies would've been fine for a normal person, but Levi had a severe food allergy. What if he was highly allergic to peanuts? Let's, for the moment, imagine he had a severe allergy to peanuts. Now, I figure that since he had such a bad allergy, he wouldn't have eaten just any cookies. I figure that they were store bought cookies that were left at his door and he knew they were ones he could eat with no problems. They didn't have anything in them that he was allergic to. They were a brand he often ate because he knew they had no peanuts in them. That's the only reason he ate them. He knew the brand."

"You're saying he died of anaphylactic shock? Is that what you're getting at? And not a heart attack?"

"That's right. I do think so."

"You might be right."

Ettie was amazed that he agreed, and kept talking. "A friend of ours was driving her buggy past Levi's house on the morning Levi died. She saw what she thought was an *Englisch* woman taking something to the house and there was a red car parked nearby. If I believed in betting, I'd bet on it that Justin disguised himself as a woman to place the lethal peanut-filled cookies on Levi's doorstep in the early hours of the morning."

"What color car does Justin drive?" Elsa-May asked the detective.

"I can't say. I only talked with him the one time, but I'll certainly talk with him and see what I can find out.

"If he was driving his own car the day we saw him and Nella at Levi's house, it would be white. But it might have been his sister's car."

Ettie resumed her tale. "When Florence left, she noticed Levi didn't look too good and that was because there was something in the cookies. They'd been tampered with. He had food intolerances—peanuts—and the taste was hidden by the chocolate. It was Justin dressed as a woman delivering the cookies to the door. That way, if anyone saw him, like they did, they would think it was a woman bringing cookies."

"Yes, I got all that the first time. Well, it's certainly a convincing story. Is that the only scenario you've concocted, Mrs. Smith, or do you have another?"

"That's all I have so far."

"I appreciate your thoughts and I'll have another talk with

Mr. Justin Bridges. How did you know about Levi's food allergy?"

Ettie looked down. "The man shelving cookies at the store mentioned a man always bought that brand—an Amish man—and he said he'd heard that the man had died recently. It had to be Levi he was talking about and the only reason Levi would've bought that brand was if he'd had food intolerances. I'm betting someone tampered with the cookies and added peanuts."

"Ettie!"

"Oh, I mean, if I was a betting person, I'd bet, but I'm not, so I won't."

Elsa-May shook her head in disgust.

Kelly nodded. "Yes, peanuts were an ingredient in the lab report of the cookies. I remember seeing that on the list and the only reason I remember that is because there weren't many ingredients. I thought nothing of peanuts being in the cookies at the time, but if what you've said is true, this could change everything. I'll go over the evidence and see if your scenario has any credence."

CHAPTER 22

*T*he next afternoon, there was a knock on their door. It was Kelly.

"Do you want a job, Mrs. Smith?"

"No."

"To do what?" Elsa-May asked as she walked up behind Ettie who was facing Kelly at the front door.

"May I come in?" he asked.

"Yes." Elsa-May gave Ettie's sleeve a tug so she'd move away from the doorway.

Ettie had no choice but to take a step back. "Let's sit in the living room." Once they were seated, Ettie asked, "Was I right about the peanuts?"

"I went over the evidence. In Levi's trash, there was a wrapper for the cookies, which we had in evidence, but the ingredients on the package didn't tally with the ingredients when the lab tested those cookies. I'm afraid to say it was something I overlooked. Since there was no poison in the cookies, it didn't occur to me to match the ingredients to those labeled on the package."

Elsa-May gasped. "Ettie, you were *right*."

Ettie pouted. "I've been right before."

"But was he allergic to peanuts like the man at the store said he was, Detective?" Elsa-May asked.

"Levi made it hard to find that out because he'd gone to a number of doctors over the years. We found a report at the local hospital from many years ago after he'd had an allergic episode. We can categorically state that he *was* allergic to peanuts."

"Ah, I *was* right."

"Good work, Ettie," Elsa-May said.

"Yes, you were, Mrs. Smith, and it was clever of you to figure that out."

Elsa-May frowned. "Don't give her too much praise, or she'll get a big head."

Ettie laughed and then stopped abruptly. "He was murdered just like he thought he'd be. Florence was right. Okay, so the cookies had peanuts in them, but who delivered them?"

Kelly crossed one leg over the other. "We're DNA testing the package. With a bit of luck, we'll find out who delivered them soon enough."

"Good," Ettie said, with a nod of her head. The way the detective was speaking, Ettie figured he once again knew more than he was letting on to them.

"Now, how about that coffee you offered me the other day?" he asked.

As Ettie listened to the click-clack of Elsa-May's knitting needles, she realized she had it all wrong.

"Ettie, get Detective Kelly something and I'll help when I finish this row."

"In a minute. I've been thinking, the nurse would've known about his food intolerances and if she was friendly with Tony, she might've let it slip. Tony tampered with those cookies and dressed himself as a woman and left them outside Levi's door in the early hours of the morning."

"What about the red car that was seen at the same time that the person was seen approaching Levi's house?" Elsa-May asked.

"The red car could've belonged to anyone."

"There's nothing around but the apple orchards."

Ettie sighed. "You're right, and since John was on a business trip... No, wait. John would've known about his father's allergy to peanuts. And that means his wife would've known as well."

"You think Levi's daughter-in-law left them on his doorstep?" Detective Kelly asked.

"There was never any eighty thousand dollars. Connie would've been able to get her hands on Levi's signature and copy it."

"What is your latest theory in total, Mrs. Smith?"

"Levi thought that the nurse stole some change he had lying around and he complained to his son about her. Connie saw that as an opportunity to find someone who would look guilty for his murder, but she had to devise a plan to increase the amount of money. That's where Eric came in with his false claim and fake paperwork."

"That makes sense. The nurse would also have looked guilty because she would've known about his peanut allergy, and everyone would've thought she took the eighty thousand dollars as well," Elsa-May said.

"Where do you think the man next door came into things?" the detective asked. "How do you think that came about?"

"Connie approached him with the plan. All he had to do was go along with the fake paperwork and pretend he had a deal with Levi and then John might have given him back the large sum of money that he said was stolen. Alternatively,

John might have sold the orchard to him much cheaper because of his deposit. The deposit that never existed in the first place."

"Ettie, are you saying that Eric knew Connie's plan to kill her father-in-law?" Elsa-May asked.

"Yes, that's exactly what I'm saying. It suited him to buy the orchard, and to do that he was happy to go along with Connie's plan. Don't forget he was furious with Levi over the loss of his organic certification."

"Why would Connie be happy to have John sell the orchard at a discount because of the eighty thousand? That's a large discount. Also, we had a theory Eric might know Nella too, but we figured it was too far-fetched. The reasoning was that Eric liked Nella, and had framed her for Levi's murder, but why would he do that? Then we dropped that theory."

Ettie shook her head at her older sister. "You've been doing too much thinking." She looked back at the detective. "Connie wouldn't have told him the whole plan. And if she did, she left out the part about Nella being the scapegoat. Connie gets what she wants—money from the sale of the orchard, and Eric gets to buy the orchard cheaper. We did have a theory about Nella and Eric, but a young woman like Nella Bridges would never have been interested in a much older man like Eric, but I suppose if she wasn't and they knew each other, he could've got annoyed when she told him so—that she wasn't interested."

"I'm not so sure we should drop that theory, Ettie." Elsa-May looked at the detective. "What do you think about that?"

"It makes some sense, in a way."

Ettie raised her eyebrows. "Really?"

"Yes and no. Part right and part wrong. Mostly you're wrong Elsa-May I'm sorry to say. We looked into Connie and John, individually and as a couple. We found out that

Connie consulted a divorce lawyer a few times over the past year. In all possibility, she could've waited until John inherited the orchard and then started divorce proceedings before he had time to gamble the money away. Or she could've had plans to control the money before he could."

"You know about the gambling?" Elsa-May asked.

"I'm a detective. We know that Eric and Levi were at odds with one another and Eric wanted to buy Levi out. How close were Eric and Connie, you ask? You might be interested to know that the phone records we obtained from Connie's personal cell phone show many calls back and forth between the pair."

Ettie gasped. "I was right!"

Kelly chuckled. "Well, let's wait until we get the DNA results from the cookie package and go from there, shall we?"

Ettie knew that Kelly wouldn't be telling them what he'd heard if he wasn't certain Connie and Eric were guilty.

TWO WEEKS LATER, Kelly visited them again. He'd stopped by the day before and asked that all three sisters be there. Ettie knew without a doubt he had wrapped up the case.

The detective sat on an old wooden chair opposite the couch where Florence and Ettie sat. Elsa-May was sitting in her usual chair.

"You have the results?" Florence asked.

He rubbed his neck, and then clasped his hands together. "We have arrested John's wife for the murder of her father-in-law."

Florence gasped. "It's true?"

"I'm afraid so. We also arrested Eric for conspiracy to commit murder."

"That's dreadful," Elsa-May said. "I can't believe it."

"Poor John. He must be devastated. When did you arrest Connie?"

"Only this morning after the DNA results came through. She tried to cut a deal with us and told us of Eric's involvement. It was convenient to have that information and no special treatment will be given to either of them."

"And what of Nella Bridges?" Ettie asked. "Where does she fit into everything?"

"I was getting to her. We finally tracked her down yesterday. She was fearful of being accused of theft and she fled, not wanting to face the pressure. We had her make a statement and that was that."

Elsa-May said. "That's understandable. She was worried because she'd been accused of something before."

"How did you know that?" Kelly asked.

"I heard a rumor."

Kelly continued, "When I told Nella about the arrests this morning, she was relieved."

Florence shook her head. "I feel sorry for John."

"Ah, yes, about John. His marriage was strained due to his wife's gambling."

"His *wife's* gambling?" Ettie asked.

"Yes, they had to sell their home to get them out of the debt she'd put them in. Now he's in disbelief that his wife could have done that to his father." Kelly looked down at the floor.

Ettie said, "At least we know what happened now."

"Yes." He nodded.

"Cup of tea or coffee, Detective?" Elsa-May asked.

He looked across at Elsa-May and said, "Surprise me."

Florence stood up. "I'll help you, Elsa-May."

When Ettie and the detective were alone, she sensed he was feeling glum. "Is there something wrong?"

He looked over at her. "It's bittersweet, Ettie. I work hard to bring justice to the families of loved ones who've been murdered, but in cases like these the resolution brings no peace. John Hochstetler's father's gone and now his wife will most likely be serving a life sentence. Where's the peace in that?"

Ettie glimpsed the compassion that Kelly had managed to conceal so cleverly behind his brash manner. He cared about people. Being a detective wasn't just a job to him. "There's no peace. John will find his peace somewhere other than this earth."

"You mean when he's dead?"

Ettie chuckled. "No, hopefully before then. In God's presence there is perfect peace."

"I hope for his sake he finds it."

"I'm certain he will. Sometimes it takes a disaster in one's life to strip us back to seeing what our true goal should be."

Florence walked out from the kitchen with a plate of food, and behind her was Elsa-May with a large pot of tea and cups and saucers.

"Here we are." Florence placed the plate on a low table in between Kelly and Ettie. "Chocolate chip cookies and chocolate covered cookies."

Kelly stared at them while Florence sat down and Elsa-May poured the tea.

"Tell me they're not the same brand of cookies?" he finally said.

"Yes, they're good for you. No gluten. The man at the store recommended them," Florence said.

He took the cup of tea Elsa-May had just poured for him. "Thank you, Mrs. Lutz."

"Won't you have a cookie?" Florence asked.

He stared at them again. "I'm not really that hungry. Just the tea will be fine for me tonight."

Ettie and Elsa-May exchanged a quiet smile.

"Are you certain?" Florence asked.

"It's a treat I'll leave for another time."

On hearing the word 'treat,' Snowy, who'd been sleeping in his dog bed in the corner, jolted his head up. When he saw his favorite detective was there, he bounded toward him.

"Oh, dear, you said the 'T' word," Elsa-May said.

Ettie reached down and managed to grab Snowy before he reached the detective, and she scooped the dog into her arms.

Kelly bounded to his feet. "I just remembered I need to fill out a report."

"Can't that wait until tomorrow?" Elsa-May said.

"I'm afraid not." On his way out, he turned to face the three sisters. "I wanted to personally let you know about the arrests."

"Thank you," Ettie said, while the others nodded agreement. Ettie glanced at both of her sisters, and then said to Kelly, "We're just having a little joke with you."

He frowned. "About what?"

Florence said, "The cookies. I baked them today myself."

Kelly looked at the three of them and then he laughed. "You had me. I can't believe you'd do that."

"Come back inside. You don't really have a report to make, do you?"

"Hmm. Homemade cookies, or doing paperwork?" He mimicked juggling motions with his hands. "It's close, but the cookies win."

Everyone laughed and Ettie took Kelly by the arm, led him back to his chair, and sat him back down.

Florence picked up the plate and handed it to him.

"They look delicious."

"And they aren't that good for you—probably."

He took a chocolate covered one as he smirked. "I didn't

know you ladies had a sense of humor. I'll have to watch you."

Seeing no one was giving him a treat, Snowy headed back to his dog bed to continue his snooze.

Elsa-May walked into the kitchen and came back out with a mug of coffee. "And here's your coffee. I know you prefer coffee rather than tea."

With his mouth full of cookie and his eyes crinkling at the corners, Detective Kelly could only nod in appreciation as he reached for the mug.

The End

Thank you for your interest in Amish Cover-Up

Other books in the Ettie Smith Amish Mysteries Series:

BOOK 1 SECRETS COME HOME

ABOUT THE AUTHOR

Samantha Price is a best selling author who knew she wanted to become a writer at the age of seven, while her grandmother read to her Peter Rabbit in the sun room. Though the adventures of Peter and his sisters Flopsy, Mopsy, and Cotton-tail started Samantha on her creative journey, it is now her love of Amish culture that inspires her to write. Her writing is clean and wholesome, with more than a dash of sweetness. Though she has penned over eighty Amish Romance and Amish Mystery books, Samantha is just as in love today with exploring the spiritual and emotional journeys of her characters as she was the day she first put pen to paper. Samantha lives in a quaint Victorian cottage with three rambunctious dogs.

www.samanthapriceauthor.com